WOMEN IN HOLLYWOOD
BOOK TWO

no one has to know

SHELIA GOSS

This work was originally published in 2015 under the title Secret Liaisons.

Cover design by Qamber Designs

Print book interior design by Qamber Designs

Honey Blossom Press
www.honeyblossompress.com
@honeyblossompress

ISBNs: 9781967565382 (trade paperback),
9781967565399 (ebook)
Printed in the United States of America

HONEY BLOSSOM PRESS

This book is dedicated to the loving memory of my father, Lloyd Goss, and my grandparents, whose lives, lessons, and love continue to guide me.

Chapter One

THIRTY-YEAR-OLD MONA JOHNSON STOOD MESMERIZED, watching her boss mingle with the actors and crew during the wrap party. Clips from the movie they'd recently filmed had just been shown, the huge cake shaped like a camera had been cut, and now everyone was drinking and having fun. Terrance Beckham's megawatt smile brightened the dimly lit room, revealing pearly-white teeth. The clean-shaven movie producer's eyes twinkled when he told jokes about things that occurred during filming. Those around him laughed, enticing Mona to move closer so she could see what all the fuss was about.

Kem Phillips, one of her best friends from college, stood next to her and said, "You did a great job organizing this party."

"Thanks, Kem. Looks like everyone is enjoying themselves," Mona responded.

"Especially those two." Kem pointed in the opposite direction.

Mona's other best friend, Charlotte Richards, stood near R&B heartthrob Sean Maxwell, who also happened to be one of the stars of the movie. Charlotte and Sean were recently engaged and were inseparable. Charlotte, an entertainment manager, was also in attendance because Terrance was one of her clients.

Mona and Kem walked through the crowd of people and stood near Charlotte and Sean.

"How's my favorite couple?" Mona asked.

"Doing great. What about you?" Charlotte responded.

"It's been fun, but I'll be glad when this night is over with," Mona said.

Sean said, "I've been telling Charlotte how great you were. Thanks for helping me get through those awkward moments."

"After this movie, you can guarantee you'll be getting other roles."

Kem said, "I might write a character for you on my show, just because."

"You ladies sure know how to make me feel good," Sean responded.

Charlotte looked at Kem. "Have your people call my people and let's make it happen."

Sean held Charlotte's hand and kissed the back of it, revealing a five-carat princess-cut diamond engagement ring. "Look at my baby, always working."

Charlotte blushed. "You are my number one client."

Sean leaned closer to Charlotte. "I better be." He brushed his lips against hers.

A young man walked over to Sean and whispered something in his ear. Sean looked at them. "Ladies, I promised this reporter an interview. Let me go take care of my obligation."

Charlotte said, "I'll tag along with you. Girls, I'll see you at the gym tomorrow."

Sean reached for Charlotte's hand. She grabbed it and they walked away from Mona and Kem.

Mona watched them as they blended into the crowd. She wanted to experience the type of love Charlotte and Sean had.

Her thoughts were interrupted with the sound of Terrance's husky voice.

"Kem, thanks for coming tonight. Mona recently shared with me that you two were good friends," Terrance said.

Kem smiled. "Yes, we've known each other since freshman year in college."

"I bet you have some stories to tell about Mona." Terrance smiled as he looked at Mona.

"She probably does." Mona winked, smiled, and continued, "But if she knows what's good for her, she'll keep them to herself, because she's a part of those stories and we wouldn't want them to get out now, would we?"

They all laughed. Terrance said, "I know I promised you tomorrow off, but an opportunity just fell into my lap. Can you be in the office by ten?"

"Sure. Anything for you," Mona said, letting her words purr as they poured out of her mouth.

Terrance smiled. "If I didn't know any better, I would think you were flirting with me."

"It must be all of the champagne you've been drinking," Mona responded.

"Must be." Terrance paused, looking at Mona and then back at Kem. "Ladies, I'll let you get back to your conversation. Kem, hope to see you again soon."

"Likewise," Kem responded.

Mona watched Terrance walk away to the other side of the room. He slipped his arm around the waist of a tall model whose name she'd purposely failed to remember. Her smile faded.

Kem cleared her throat. "What's wrong?"

"Not a thing. Terrance is a nice person, but he's always with a different woman." Mona grabbed a flute of champagne from the waiter walking by.

"Why is that your concern? He's a grown man. And the women don't seem to mind," Kem said.

"If it wasn't for that, I could see—" Mona stopped herself before completing her sentence. "Never mind. Let me go check on the catering company. Looks like we're running out of some things."

"I'll wait to hang out with Charlotte and Sean while you do that," Kem said.

Mona took a quick drink of her champagne and placed it on a table. While everyone else partied, She made sure everything went well.

Terrance noticed Mona pass him out of the corner of his eye. It was hard not to notice her in the bright red dress. He admired how the formfitting dress fell over her petite, slender body, accenting her small waist and round butt. His mind drifted to places it shouldn't.

The date he'd forgotten about tapped him on the arm.

"Why are you watching her when I'm standing right here?" Bambi asked.

She didn't try to pressure him into a relationship like some other women, which was the only reason Terrance had invited her. She also wasn't too bright, but she made for good eye candy.

"I don't know what you're talking about," Terrance responded. He turned and faced her.

"Is this party almost over? Because I'm ready to go. I got off the plane and came straight here." She looked irritated.

Terrance said, "Why don't you go to your hotel and wait for my call?"

Bambi's tone changed and got a little louder. "Are you dismissing me?"

Terrance was a movie producer and loved drama, but on the screen, not in his own personal life. Bambi had just officially axed herself from his calling list. "Can you keep it down?"

"No. I flew from New York to Los Angeles just to be with you tonight, and you're going to try to dismiss me because you have the hots for someone else? No, that's not going to happen."

People started looking in their direction. Terrance wanted to go hide behind a camera. Mona walked back in the room and straight to where he and Bambi stood.

"Bam, I mean Bambi, I think it's time for you to leave. You have a good reputation and you really don't want the gossip blogs to be talking about how you caused a scene at tonight's wrap party, now do you? I heard you got a new contract with Motives Cosmetics, and I'm sure there's a morality clause in there, so let's not jeopardize that."

Bambi scowled and looked at Terrance. "You better be glad your assistant knows what she's talking about, or else I would slap you right now. Lose my number and forget you ever knew me." She put a fake smile on her face and sashayed out of the room as if she hadn't just caused a disturbance.

Mona turned to the crowd, who had gone silent to watch the scene. "The party's not over. Deejay, crank the music up."

People around them ignored the disturbance and went back to enjoying the festivities. Terrance was glad the attention was no longer on him.

He said to Mona, "Thanks for coming to my rescue."

"Anytime, boss," she responded, and then walked away.

Terrance saw a group of actors who were in his latest film. He plastered a smile on his face and went to mingle with the cast. He pushed the incident with Bambi to the back of his mind but couldn't keep his thoughts off Mona.

Chapter Two

MONA MET WITH CHARLOTTE AND Kem early the next morning at the gym. They discussed the events from the previous night as they worked out.

Mona said, "Ms. Bambi walked her not-so-happy behind out of there."

Kem, who walked on the treadmill, said, "I'm sure you enjoyed that, didn't you?"

"Every minute of it." Mona stopped pedaling the stationary bike.

"I was standing nearby. She was complaining about being tired, so Terrance told her to go," Charlotte said as she wiped the sweat from her brow with her towel. "And that's when she went off."

"One thing I've learned from working for Terrance is that he doesn't like scenes," Mona said. "Ms. Model wanted to embarrass him with her outburst, but it backfired on her. She didn't get the response from Sean she wanted. That's why she was so upset."

"From the looks of it, you're probably right," Charlotte said.

"I'm sure you're happy about that," Kem replied.

Mona looked at Kem. "You keep implying something, but I'm going to ignore you."

"I call it like I see it."

"Am I missing something?" Charlotte asked.

"Our friend, the same one who complains about her boss, really likes him, if you catch my drift." Kem smiled.

"Don't listen to her. She's writing a fantasy in her head and trying to make me the star." Mona got off the bike and moved on to the treadmill. "Besides, Terrance is the last man I would choose to be with."

"Kem, Mona has a point," Charlotte said. "We both have seen Terrance at events around town. Can you name a time you've seen him with the same woman twice?"

Kem looked in the air as if she were thinking.

"Case closed," Mona said. "The man for me will be ready for a commitment. Not someone who gets off by dating multiple women."

Charlotte said, "There are plenty of men out there, so you'll find someone."

"Lately, most of the men I meet are only after my assets—and I emphasize the *ass* part. They aren't looking to get past my looks to find out who I am."

"That's why I'm concentrating on building my empire. I'm tired of the rat race," Kem said.

"I want to be in a relationship, but with the right man. Someone who likes the same things I like, someone who isn't trying to be a player. Does Sean have any brothers?" Mona jokingly asked.

"I must say, my baby is one in a million. I can't tell you how happy he's made me. He doesn't try to change me. He accepts me and loves me just the way I am." Charlotte's smile grew large.

"I want what you and Sean have," Mona confessed.

"If it were up to me, both of my best friends would be just as happy as I am," Charlotte said. Her phone beeped. She pulled it out of her pocket and read the text message. "Ladies, I have to cut this short. One of my clients has gotten themselves into a bind." She grabbed her things and left.

Mona increased the speed on the treadmill as Kem said, "If you're serious about meeting someone, I may have a solution to your dilemma."

"What's that?"

"My cousin's sorority sister Rowena has a dating site called 2-of-a-Kind."

Mona stopped the treadmill. "Meeting men isn't the problem. Meeting the *right* man is my issue."

"That's just it. Most of the people who use the site are professional people just like you. You have to fill out an extensive questionnaire, and the database pairs you with a match based on the information you entered."

"If it's so good, then why haven't you used it?" Mona asked.

"Because I'm not looking to be in a relationship," Kem responded.

"What's the name of the site again? I guess it doesn't hurt to try it."

Kem repeated the dating site information, and Mona made a mental note to visit it later.

"I guess I better go shower and change. I don't want to keep my boss waiting," Mona said.

"You could always bypass the site and stop fighting your attraction to Terrance," Kem said.

"There you go again. I will let you know how things go with 2-of-a-Kind," Mona said as she hopped off the treadmill and headed to the locker room to shower and change.

Terrance leaned back in his black leather chair behind his desk and listened to his mother go on and on about how much she was ready for him to settle down and give her grandbabies while she was still young enough to enjoy them.

"I'm not getting any younger," Sara Beckham said.

"I know, Mom. When I meet the right woman, I do plan to marry her and give you all the grandchildren you want," Terrance said. He'd said it before, but to ease her mind, he didn't mind repeating himself.

"Before you go making any type of commitment, the woman must pass my inspection," she said.

Terrance laughed. "Mom, all that should matter is the fact that I love her."

"I see the women you're always with. They're all gold diggers. You need a good, wholesome woman. Someone who won't be after you because of your money."

Terrance swiveled his chair around when he heard his office door open. Mona stood in the doorway in a midnight-blue pantsuit and white blouse. It didn't matter what she wore—she could not hide her well-toned body.

"Mom, I've got to go. I'll call you back tonight, I promise."

"Don't forget what I told you. No more gold diggers," Sara said. "And you need to do something about that assistant of yours. She never passes my calls through."

"Bye, Mom," Terrance said, and disconnected the call.

"You didn't have to hang up on my account," Mona said as she walked in.

"I was looking for an excuse to get off the phone. As always, you saved me."

She crossed her arms and smiled. "Sounds like I should be getting a raise."

"I'll think about it," Terrance said. "Have a seat."

Mona took a seat in front of his desk. "Do I need my recorder for this?"

"You're fine."

She placed her iPad on his desk and gave him her undivided attention.

The whiff of Mona's sweet floral fragrance made him want to get closer. He pushed his chair back some. He needed to shake whatever feeling he was having. Last night he'd dreamed of her in the red dress. He'd imagined her removing the dress, slowly, and now this morning, he wanted to get close to her. Mona was off-limits. She was his employee.

"You zoned out. Do you want to call this meeting for another time?" Mona asked.

"No. I'll be all right." Terrance needed to pull himself together. "Charlotte has gotten me a meeting with some network executives, and they are interested in me pitching a couple of TV pilots to them. If this works out, this will be my first TV show. My dilemma is that I have to narrow it down to three. We've gotten a lot of submissions, and I need you to help me determine which three to go with."

"What about your assistant producer?" Mona asked.

"As of last night, he will no longer be working with me. He's decided to take a position with the *Night Show* on CBS, so he's leaving tomorrow."

"I hate to see Bill go. I like him."

"Me too. Not only do I have to find a script, but a new assistant producer."

"I think both of our dilemmas have been solved. I need a raise to help me pay my bills, and you need an assistant producer. In the past, the assistant producer has helped you with reading scripts, and that's what you just asked me to do."

"That means we'll be working together even more than we are now," Terrance said.

"I don't have a problem with that, unless you do." Mona batted her beautiful, long black eyelashes and eased back in her chair.

"There's no problem at all," Terrance said, shifting in his seat when Mona licked her bottom lip.

She's your employee, Terrance told himself over and over as he tried to get the visual of Mona licking her lip out of his head.

Chapter Three

MONA LIVED IN A SMALL, quaint apartment located above an elderly couple's house. She carried her small bag of groceries up the stairs. Although her neighborhood was nice, it was nowhere near as luxurious as the ones Kem and Charlotte lived in.

She had been grateful when she came across the rental while searching online one day. It was an upgrade from where she'd stayed before, but not by much. She normally chose to visit Kem and Charlotte at their places because sometimes she was embarrassed by her small living quarters.

Being a teacher didn't pay much, and her moonlighting as a production assistant soon paid off when she landed the job as Terrance's full-time assistant. She'd quit teaching English at Los Angeles Middle Prep School and taken the job. It didn't pay but five thousand dollars more, but she was closer to her dream of being a professional screenwriter.

This wasn't how she'd originally planned her life. By now, she was supposed to be married to Garrett Maywood, her college sweetheart. People used to call them M&M because during their college years they were inseparable. That was, until the day Mona learned from Garrett's mom that he'd moved on without her. He hadn't the heart to tell her he wanted to break it off with her, so he sent his mother to do the deed.

His mom never liked her anyway, because Mona came from humble beginnings. She'd grown up in the Dallas area, and although she never wanted for anything, her parents weren't rich. Mona's grades were good throughout high school. If it weren't for her fully paid scholarship, she wouldn't have been able to attend the University of California.

Kem was correct when she said Mona was attracted to Terrance, but Mona knew not to cross the line with her boss. Terrance was the love-them-and-leave-them type. Sure, she could probably entice him into bed, but she wouldn't act on her emotions and jeopardize her job, especially now.

With her new responsibilities, she hoped Terrance gave her a raise. She could picture herself moving out of the small apartment into something much bigger and nicer.

She'd bought most of her furniture from an estate sale, so although it looked expensive, she'd barely paid anything for it. The only thing she did splurge on was her mattress. She bought it brand new.

She placed her huge handbag on the sofa then put the groceries she'd just purchased in the refrigerator.

After taking a long, hot bath and cooking a quick meal, Mona crossed her legs on the couch and opened her handbag. She placed several of the scripts she needed to read next to her. She looked at the first one and read the first ten pages, and then the last ten pages. She put it in the "maybe" pile. She did the same thing with the next script and placed it in the "reject" pile. It took her five scripts before she found even one that she felt would be a good series. Several hours later, she'd narrowed it down to two, but Terrance wanted three.

The last script was terrible. It was definitely going in the "reject" pile. She looked at the "maybe" pile and picked one up, then placed it back down. She retrieved her iPad from her purse and scrolled through her files until she came to one of her own scripts. It was about three single sisters who were forced to live with each other after the death of their mother in order to gain their inheritance. It was a sexy drama that was better than any of the scripts in the "maybe" pile. She printed out the one-hour pilot episode, but before doing that, she changed the writer's name to a pen name—Sparkle.

Satisfied that she'd now chosen three good scripts for Terrance, she finally went to bed.

Terrance tossed and turned in his king-sized bed the majority of the night. Unable to sleep, he turned on the television. He flipped stations until he came across a commercial with an attractive couple talking about how they met on a dating website called 2-of-a-Kind. Terrance listened to the commercial and became curious. He made a mental note of the site. He just might check it out. He wouldn't tell anyone, because of course no one would think he needed to be on a dating site.

The more Terrance thought about the site, the more he liked the idea. With it, he could remain anonymous. He could actually see if the women he met wanted to meet him because of the man he was on the inside, not because of his financial status or what they thought he could do for their career.

He found himself getting sleepy, but made a mental note to create a membership soon. 2-of-a-Kind could solve two of his problems. It could help get his mom off his back, and it could help him push thoughts of Mona in sexual positions from his head.

Terrance drifted off to sleep, then felt lips on top of his. He opened his eyes, and Mona straddled him wearing nothing but sheer lingerie.

"What are you doing?" he asked.

She silenced him by kissing him again. "Do you want me to stop?" she asked.

"No," Terrance responded, barely above a whisper.

Mona eased out of her panties, and before Terrance could blink, she was riding him. He watched with delight as she moaned out his name over and over.

He took one of her nipples in his mouth and felt her bounce on him. They held each other tight as she climaxed.

Terrance eased Mona off him, and she lay on her back. The moisture between her legs excited him as he thrust inside of her. He could no longer control himself and released inside of her, bringing them both to a climax.

The alarm clock buzzed at the exact same moment he climaxed and woke Terrance out of his wet dream.

Chapter Four

TERRANCE WALKED IN TO HIS office wearing shades. Not because he was trying to be cool but to hide the bags under his eyes from the lack of sleep. After waking from his wet dream, he'd hit the shower and stayed there until the water ran cold.

He wished he could avoid seeing Mona today. He felt embarrassed for thinking of her in the way that he had. *It was just a dream,* he told himself as he neared her.

"Hi, boss," she said in her soft, sweet voice. "I put the three scripts on your desk."

Terrance didn't trust his voice. He nodded instead to acknowledge he'd heard her and went straight to his office. He needed to get a grip on himself. He was not his normal, cool self. He told himself again, *It was just a dream.*

He removed his shades and sat behind his desk. He needed to concentrate on work. He sent an email to Mona and asked her to hold all of his calls. For the next few hours, he read the scripts and Mona's notes on each one. He narrowed his choices down to two. One would be a thirty-minute sitcom and the other a one-hour drama. He called Mona into his office.

Wearing a fitted navy-blue dress suit, she waltzed into his office and stood in front of him.

"Have a seat. I've narrowed my choices down to two."

"Which ones?" Mona sat. She crossed her legs, revealing her shapely thighs.

Terrance cleared his throat. "The family comedy and the family drama."

Mona smiled. "Great. Instead of choosing which one, why don't you present both?"

Terrance thought about it. She was right. It was best to be prepared to pitch both shows than to pitch one before they mentioned they were no longer looking for that genre.

"What I need for you to do is to get in contact with the writers so I can offer them an option," Terrance said.

He handed her the two scripts just as the office phone rang.

Mona hit the speaker button and answered, "TNB Productions, this is Mona, how may I help you?"

"Put my son on the phone," Terrance's mom said in a rude voice.

"Ms. Sara, he's actually right here."

"Good. I bet you didn't even tell him I called earlier."

Mona whispered, "I'm sorry. I forgot."

"No biggie," Terrance said. "Mom, I'm right here. What's so urgent that you couldn't wait for me to return your call?"

Mona sighed with relief.

"A mom can't call to check on her boy?"

"No, Mom, there's nothing wrong with that." Terrance picked up the handset.

Mona stood. With the scripts in her hand, she waved at Terrance and left to give him some privacy.

"Mom, I hope you know you were on speaker. I heard how rude you were to Mona. You can't be talking to her like that," he said.

"If you hired someone more competent, then we wouldn't be having this problem."

"Mona's great. She takes real good care of me," Terrance said.

"I'm sure she does. I'm sure that's the only reason why you keep her around."

"There's nothing going on between Mona and me. She's a great assistant, and I'm thinking about giving her a promotion."

"I guess if I was a woman trying to work my way into Hollywood, I would use my ass, I mean *assets*, to get ahead too."

"Mom, seriously, you got the wrong idea. It's strictly business between us, and that's not going to change."

"Make sure it doesn't."

"Was there anything else you needed to talk about? Because I have a luncheon I almost forgot about," Terrance said.

"No, dear. I just wanted to hear my favorite son's voice."

Terrance laughed. "I'm your only son."

"You're still my favorite. Go. I'll talk with you later."

Just like that, Sara dismissed Terrance. He hoped he'd cleared things up with his mom about Mona.

Mona's smile remained on her face as she sat behind her desk. She was thrilled Terrance liked her script. She found herself in a dilemma because he didn't really know it was her script. She got her phone out to call Charlotte for advice, but then stopped. Charlotte was Terrance's manager, so Mona didn't want to put her in the middle of her situation. She called Kem instead.

"You caught me right before I was getting ready for our table read. What's up?" Kem asked.

"Terrance has a pitch meeting with one of the networks, and he's chosen my script to pitch," Mona said.

"That's great news. I'm happy for you."

"The only thing is, he doesn't know it's my script. I used a pen name so he wouldn't."

"That's fine. But you know he's going to need to know it's you. He can't pitch the idea without optioning the script. Your real name has to be on the legal papers in order for him to do that."

"I know. I just wish I could prolong him finding out it was me… Well, at least until after he knows whether they will go with the idea or not."

"Which network will he be pitching to?" Kem asked.

"Not sure. He hadn't revealed that to me yet."

"Find out. If it's with my network, you know I'll put in a good word. I'm excited for you. This could be your big break," Kem said.

Mona could feel her friend's genuine excitement over the phone. "I'm going to go confess that it's me. If he changes his mind about pitching my show, then so be it."

"He won't. Oh, before I go, have you signed up for 2-of-a-Kind yet? One of my crew members just announced their engagement. And it was with a man she met on the site."

"I got busy with work, but I will," Mona said.

"People are coming in now. Chat with you later."

Kem hung up. Mona sighed out loud. Terrance walked to her desk just as she ended her call.

"I'm glad you're here," she said. "I have a confession to make."

"Please don't tell me you're quitting on me," Terrance said.

"Oh no. I wouldn't do that," Mona said. "It's about the scripts."

"Whew. I couldn't bear to lose two of you in one week."

"It's about the writers," she said.

"Were you able to reach them?" Terrance asked.

"I'm waiting to hear from the one who wrote the comedy."

"What about this Sparkle? Is she willing to sign the option agreement?" Terrance asked.

"After she has her attorney look at it, she will. But Sparkle is the reason why I wanted to talk to you. I sort of know this Sparkle."

"That's a good thing. If her script gets picked by the network, it's a great opportunity for her, and we can all make money. Let her know I'm not trying to cheat her out of anything," Terrance said.

"Oh, she knows that, because Sparkle is me."

"And let her know…" Terrance stopped mid-sentence. "Wait a minute. Did you just say *you* were Sparkle?"

"Yes," Mona said. She looked away.

"I loved the script. Why didn't you tell me that? Had me thinking it was someone else."

"I didn't think you would read it if you knew I wrote it. Besides, you said pick three scripts, and I felt guilty including mine along with the other two."

"Do you mean you've been working with me for this past year and haven't shared any of your work before? What else do you have? Besides pitching the series, I'm looking to see what I want my next feature film to be."

Mona was amazed. She hadn't gotten the negative response she thought she would get from Terrance. He seemed excited to learn she was the screenwriter. Kem was right. Even if the network passed on her series, this could be the opportunity she'd dreamed of.

"I do have other scripts. Tell me what kind of story you're looking for and I can let you know if I have something that might work for you." Mona found herself rambling.

"I have a luncheon to attend. But later, let's talk." Terrance smiled at her.

"Yes, let's talk."

Mona watched Terrance leave. She got out of her seat and did her happy dance. Then she sat back behind her computer but couldn't stop smiling.

Chapter Five

MONA FELT LIKE CELEBRATING. SHE sent messages to Charlotte and Kem, but they both had previous engagements so weren't available to celebrate with her tonight.

Terrance called and said that he was working from home the remainder of the day. Mona, a little disappointed about not having anyone to share her good news with, opened the browser on her laptop.

"I'm tired of being by myself," Mona said out loud as she typed in the URL for 2-of-a-Kind.

The website came up. Mona created a profile. She contemplated on a user name. She typed in, *Raven*. It captured her vibrant personality and kept her anonymous until she felt comfortable revealing her real name to any prospective dates.

Filling out the profile wasn't as quick and simple as Mona thought it would be. Some of the questions delved into her psyche. She felt like she was back in school writing a thesis as she answered the questions. One was, *How do you feel about commitment?*

She typed, *I am looking for total commitment from a man. He should be loyal and trustworthy. If he's not ready to make a full commitment, then I am not the woman for him. I am not looking for a booty call. I want a man who is willing to take the time to get to know me. A man who I can build a future with.*

Some of the questions only required her to hit the agree or disagree button. She laughed when she read the statement *Couples do not need to have a passionate sex life to be happy.* Right next to the statement there were two boxes, *Agree* or *Disagree*. She wished there were several disagreement buttons. Passion was a necessity.

She had to choose six words or phrases to describe her personality. She chose *vibrant, easygoing, kind, honest, hardworking,* and *a good sense of humor.*

It took her two hours to finish her profile. The site didn't require her to upload any photos. It wanted to match couples based purely on the data they entered. Mona hit the save button. She glanced at the clock and saw that it was nearly four in the afternoon. Hopefully, by the time she made it home, the site would have sent her a few matches to check out.

Terrance decided not to return to the office after the luncheon. Lately, being around Mona had his hormones jumping all over the place. He'd been disciplined in that area for so long, so this new feeling caught him by surprise.

With her revelation that she was the writer of the script that he wanted to pitch to the networks, he definitely needed to get his mind refocused. As soon as he got to his two-story home in Baldwin Hills, he headed to his den and turned on the computer.

He was on a mission to find a woman. He created a profile on 2-of-a-Kind. Some of the questions seemed a little too personal, but he wanted to find the right matches, so he answered them as truthfully as he could.

One of the questions asked him how he felt about keeping secrets. He responded, *There should be no secrets between me and the person I'm with. Trust and loyalty are two important qualities that I must have with any woman I plan to commit to.*

Terrance thought back to his college sweetheart, Nikki Reed. To his mother's dismay, he'd broken it off with Nikki when he found out she'd been secretly dating his best friend. He also found out that she was only with him because he came from an affluent family and she liked the *perks* of being his girlfriend.

His desire to be with one woman was halted by not just Nikki but other women he'd met over the years. Those women were more impressed with his bank account or his occupation than him. He felt it was safe to date multiple women because he didn't want to fall in love again and be hurt the way Nikki had hurt him all those years ago.

He'd had every intention of proposing to Nikki. He stopped by to surprise her with a ring, but he was the one who got surprised when he found her straddling Doug White, his best friend since elementary school.

That day not only ended their relationship but his lifelong friendship with Doug. He never told his mom the real reason he broke things off with Nikki. Nikki lied about who her parents were. She lied about a lot of things. He could have gotten past those things, but she'd also lied about loving him.

He hadn't been in a committed relationship since her, and he felt it was time to change that.

Terrance completed the profile questions. He emphasized that some of the traits for a potential partner must include compassion, honesty, and being ready to make a full commitment.

He hit the save button. Terrance hoped the last few hours he'd spent filling out the profile would result in his finding his soul mate—or at the very least, an interesting date.

Chapter Six

MONA CURLED UP ON THE couch and logged on to 2-of-a-Kind. The icon blinked, indicating there were several matches. She opened each profile. She was a little disappointed that none of the matches were with men who lived nearby. Most of them were located either on the East Coast or in the South. She contemplated whether to update the location requirement for her ideal mate, but didn't want to limit herself. It was possible her soul mate lived elsewhere, so she vowed to have an open mind.

She was about to log off when her computer beeped. The site indicated that there was an incoming match. The name on the profile was *Falcon*. She smiled when she saw that he lived in the Los Angeles area. She read the profile. On paper, the man seemed perfect for her. At the end of his profile, there was an option to send a personal message.

Mona typed, *Your profile caught my attention. I wanted to reach out to you to show my interest.*

Falcon responded immediately, *Thanks for reaching out. After reading your profile, I'm curious to find out how compatible we really are.*

Mona, excited and surprised by his quick response, typed, *There's only one way to find out.*

Falcon responded, *Why did you choose the profile name Raven?*

It describes my independent personality. It's also a name that has a quiet strength to it, Mona typed.

Interesting, Falcon responded.

What about you? Why Falcon?

Do you really want to know?

Yes.

Because Falcon is an African American superhero from the comics I read as a child. It also describes me because, as an African American man, I've had many obstacles to overcome in order to succeed in life. I think I can soar as high as a falcon when I put my mind to it. He ended his statement with a smiley face.

I like your attitude, Mona typed.

She and Falcon chatted back and forth during the course of the next hour. They talked about their favorite music artists and movies. They disagreed on which *Friday* movie was the funniest.

Mona yawned. She glanced at the bottom right-hand side of her laptop and noticed the time. It was after eleven. She was sleepy but didn't want to end the conversation.

She typed, *I hate to go, but I have a boss who can be demanding, so I need to get my rest.*

Falcon responded, *If I'm not being too forward, what's your email address? I would like to continue chatting throughout the day.*

Mona wasn't sure she was ready to give him her personal email. *We can chat. I'll make sure I stay logged in so I won't miss your messages.*

I understand. Look to hear from me tomorrow. Good night, Falcon responded.

Good night.

She logged off the site and got ready for bed. She went to sleep hopeful that she'd made a connection.

Terrance smiled as he logged off. Raven seemed like a nice woman. Based on the way she answered her questions on her profile, she was ideal for him. He enjoyed the playful banter they'd exchanged. One of the things he really liked was that she enjoyed his love of the arts.

He found himself trying to visualize how she looked. The only downfall to the site was that there were no pictures included with the profiles. He'd started to ask her for one but knew if he did, he would have to present one of *his* pictures to her. Although he wasn't an actor, his face was well known due to the success of the movies he produced.

He wasn't conceited, but he also knew that he was an attractive man, and pictures of his dates with beautiful women seemed to always make the gossip sites.

Keeping his anonymity for now was very important. He needed to make sure the woman on the other end of the computer cared about what was on the inside of him versus what she'd read about him.

When the site came back with the matches, he'd read them all, but Raven caught his attention more than the others. While the others came back with no higher than an eighty-five percent match, Raven was ninety percent.

Before he could respond to her, she'd messaged him. He went to bed thinking about Raven. She was nice, but he'd already found the woman he wanted.

He just wished he could do something about it.

He drifted off to sleep with Mona on his mind.

Chapter Seven

MONA'S RIDE INTO THE OFFICE took longer than usual due to a traffic accident, but it didn't mar her attitude. The good mood she was in after chatting with Falcon the night before lingered into daylight.

Terrance hadn't made it into the office yet, so Mona got behind her computer and logged in to her 2-of-a-Kind account. Her smile turned into a frown. Her inbox was empty. She'd hoped that she would have heard from Falcon by now, but she reminded herself that it was still early. It wasn't even nine o'clock.

She minimized the browser and went through her normal morning routine of making sure hot coffee was brewed for Terrance. Afterward, she skimmed through emails and voicemails. She responded to most of the messages in her inbox. There were a few requiring Terrance's attention. She forwarded him those and made a note to tell him about them.

The sound of her cell phone ringing broke her momentum. Charlotte's name showed on the display. Mona had barely answered before she heard Charlotte say, "Why am I the last person to find out that your script was chosen by Terrance for his pitching session?"

"I was going to tell you, but I know Terrance is one of your clients, so I didn't want there to be any sort of conflict," Mona confessed.

"I'm your friend first, a talent manager second. After I broker this deal for him, all of us must get together and celebrate. This is your big break, and I'm so happy for you."

"Kem said the same thing, but it hasn't happened yet."

"Aren't you the one whose always hollering, 'Think positive'? Well, I'm telling you, think positive. It's going to happen," Charlotte said, excitement in her voice.

"Speaking of your client, he just walked in the door, so I'll call you back later," Mona said, then ended her call with Charlotte.

"Good morning, sunshine," Terrance said as he walked in and went straight to his office.

Mona looked at him curiously. He'd never called her "sunshine." She placed the notepad under her arm and went to pour him a cup of coffee. She added one packet of sugar and a little cream, just like he preferred, and took it to him.

Terrance was typing something on his laptop when she entered. He stopped for a second but barely looked at her.

"Here's your coffee," she said.

"You can put it down. I'll get it in a minute," he responded.

Mona walked around to place it near him. Terrance closed his laptop. He looked at her and smiled, then picked up the coffee and took a sip.

"Just the way I like it," he commented.

Mona removed the pad from under her arm and tore off the top sheet of paper. "You got a few calls that require your attention. And also, check your email."

"I don't know what I would do without you."

"Let's hope you never have to find out," Mona said. She turned and walked out.

She went back to her desk and opened the browser. She smiled when she noticed the message from Falcon.

Terrance drank more of his coffee before opening his laptop. He didn't want anyone, especially Mona, to know that he was using a dating site.

He saw that Raven had responded to his good-morning message. *Good morning. I thought about you too.*

Terrance typed, *I have a busy day ahead of me, but know that I will be thinking of you. Until tonight, have a good day.*

I will now that I've heard from you. Enjoy the rest of your day.

Terrance logged out of his account and looked at the sheet of paper with the notes Mona had given him, then went through his normal routine of responding to emails and returning phone calls. When he finished, he summoned Mona to his office.

She walked in looking jovial, a huge smile on her face. The sight of her standing there in a royal-blue jumpsuit made his heart flutter.

"What do you need, boss?" she asked.

"Are you busy tonight?" Terrance asked.

"Why?" Mona walked closer to his desk.

"Charlotte just informed me that we were invited to a party. Some of the executives from the network will be there, and since you're one of the writers and my acting co-producer, I wanted to see if you were available to tag along."

"Yes, I'm available. What time do you want me to be there?"

"It starts at seven. I'll pick you up at six."

"I think it's best I meet you there," Mona said.

"Are you sure? Because I have no problem driving to the Valley."

"Just give me the address."

"Let's compromise. Why don't we leave from here?"

"Do you see what I have on?" Mona indicated her jumpsuit.

Terrance bit his bottom lip. He didn't see anything wrong with her attire. Nothing at all.

He reached into his pocket and pulled out his wallet, removing a credit card and handing it to her. "Take a late lunch. This is an important event for the both of us, so find something nice to wear."

"What's my limit?"

"I'm going to leave it to your discretion. Don't get carried away, but buy whatever you want. I look at this as an investment in our future."

Mona walked toward the door, stopped, and turned around. "Remember, you said to get what I want."

Terrance laughed. "I sure did, and I hope I don't regret it."

"You won't. Trust me." Mona winked and walked out.

Chapter Eight

MONA WENT SHOPPING AT A nearby mall. She found the perfect dress, shoes, and accessories for tonight's event. The door to the office was locked when she returned. She struggled to hold her items as she fumbled in her purse for her set of keys.

Once inside, she hung the garment bag and placed the other shopping bags near it.

She noticed a yellow sticky note on her computer. It read, *Will be back later. The other writer called. We're all set.*

Mona's phone rang. She saw her attorney's name and number displayed on the screen. "Hi," she answered.

"Mona, this is Blythe Evans—I went over the option agreement and I only made a few changes. I've emailed it to you. Call me back when you get it so we can discuss."

"If you have a minute, we can discuss it now." Mona sat behind her computer and logged on. She opened the Word document and read over the highlighted changes.

"If they want your story idea, I want to make sure you're listed as the head writer," Blythe said.

"I'm reading through this, and it sounds perfect. I hope Terrance agrees to the changes."

"If it works for you, I'll email you the document without the markups and all you'll need to do is print it, sign it, and hand it back to Terrance."

Fifteen minutes later, Mona did just as her attorney said. She printed out two copies and signed each one. She placed them both in a manila folder—all she needed to do now was wait for Terrance to come back to the office.

She hoped she didn't get any resistance to her changes. The original contract was fair, but the updated one ensured that she would play an important role if her script was chosen.

Terrance walked in holding two brown bags. "Hey, you're back. I figured you didn't have time to buy lunch, so I got us both something from the Chinese restaurant down the street."

"Perfect," Mona said. She stood and took one of the bags from him.

"Did you have any luck finding a dress?" he asked.

"Yes. Thank you again." She reached into her purse and pulled out his credit card, then handed it to him.

"Well, where is it? Where's the dress?"

"No can do. You will see it when I put it on."

"Come on. I need to see what my money bought."

"Your food's getting cold. And you know it's not going to taste the same cold, so I suggest you eat it while it's still hot," Mona playfully said as she shooed Terrance toward his office.

"Fine. I guess I can wait."

"Don't worry, it'll be worth it."

Terrance went to his office but left his door open. Mona held the manila folder with her signed contracts and joined him soon afterward.

"Here's the signed option agreement with a few changes. Hope it's to your satisfaction." She placed the folder on Terrance's desk.

"I'll take a look at it as soon as I finish eating," he responded.

"Great. Now let me get back to my shrimp fried rice." Mona left out that she hoped Terrance agreed to her changes.

After finishing his food and wiping his hands clean, Terrance opened the manila folder and read through the contract. If it had been anyone else but Mona, he would have been hesitant in signing the contract with the changes, but he wanted the best for her and didn't have a problem bringing her on as head writer if the network agreed to the production.

He signed both copies. He kept one in the folder and took the other to Mona.

"Mona, as the owner of TNB Productions, I hope that our relationship will be taken to another level with this new venture." He handed her the contract.

Mona looked at his signature on the bottom of the second page and smiled. "So we have a deal?"

"Yes, we do. Tonight's a prelude to our meeting, so let's knock it out of the park."

"Thank you so much. I'll never forget this." Mona jumped out of her seat and hugged Terrance.

He could smell the sweet aroma of flowers in her long, curled hair. He wrapped his arm around her, enjoying the closeness.

Mona slowly pulled away, but not before they both stared into each other's eyes longer than they normally would have. She said, "I'm sorry. I just got a little emotional. You don't know how bad I want this to work."

"No need to apologize. I'm excited for you. I'm glad that I can hopefully be a part of making your dream come true."

"You have. More than you'll ever know," Mona said as she sat back down.

Terrance stared at her. She was petite but full of life. Being around her energized him, made him feel as if he could do anything.

He went back to his office and turned on the radio. Erykah Badu's "Next Lifetime" came on. He thought of Mona. Maybe if circumstances were different, he could envision himself with her. But with this possible upcoming production, any thoughts of a romantic encounter with her needed to be pushed out of his mind.

He hopped on the dating site and sent Raven a quick, short message. He needed a distraction from Mona, and chatting with Raven was just the solution.

Chapter Nine

MONA ENDED THE CHAT WITH Falcon so she could get ready for the dinner party. To her surprise, Terrance stayed in his office behind closed doors the remainder of the day. He hadn't asked her to do anything for him, so she was free to chat online.

She took her dress and other items and went to the bathroom. She freshened up and got dressed. She pinned back her black hair, leaving bangs and a few loose strands on the side. She placed on a pair of faux-diamond earrings and matching necklace. She slipped into the emerald-green, knee-length evening dress with the spaghetti straps revealing her light-brown back. She bent and placed on a pair of black, velvet-smooth heels with diamond accents.

Satisfied with her appearance, she walked out of the bathroom holding a bag with her other clothes in it. She placed the bag under her desk and glanced at the clock on the wall. It was nearing six o'clock. She knocked on Terrance's door.

"I'll be out in a minute. I'm getting dressed," he yelled from the other side.

"Okay. I'm ready when you are," Mona yelled back.

She went to make sure all of the electric equipment such as her computer and coffeemaker were turned off.

"You look beautiful," Terrance said when she turned around to face him. He stood just outside of his office looking at her.

She felt a little uncomfortable because she thought she saw desire in his eyes. She wished she had a shawl to cover her arms so he couldn't see the chill bumps that swept over her skin when she heard his voice.

She twirled so he could get the full effect. "You like?"

"Thumbs-up. You're going to make the other women envious."

"Thanks to you." Mona smiled.

"You must have gotten that dress on sale, because you look like a million bucks. I saw the receipt. It didn't cost nearly as much as it looks."

"It just so happened to be on the clearance rack."

"Any other woman would have bought the most expensive dress in the store, but not you. I can't complain, but you could have spent more if you wanted to," Terrance said, walking closer.

"You did say, 'Get the dress you wanted,' right?" Mona asked.

"I sure did."

"This emerald dress was what I wanted. Besides, you were doing something nice for me. I wasn't going to take advantage of your generosity."

"Mona Johnson, you always amaze me," Terrance said.

"Let's do this," she said.

Terrance held out his arm, and Mona placed her hand on it. "Our chariot awaits," he said.

He led her outside. Mona's eyes widened when she saw the black stretch limousine waiting for them in the parking lot. The driver held the door open, and they entered the car.

Terrance poured them each a flute of champagne and held his glass in the air to toast. "To our new partnership. May this be the start of many more to come."

"I'll drink to that." Mona tapped her glass with his and then took a sip of the champagne.

Terrance gave her a quick rundown on some of the people who were to be at the dinner party. "If you're unsure of what to say, just smile and I'll take over from there."

"Well, you know me. Shyness has never been one of my problems."

"You do have the gift of gab," Terrance said.

"So stop worrying. I want this to happen as much as you do."

Mona placed her hand on top of Terrance's. His eyes softened. He reached over and kissed her. Not a simple peck on the lips, but the kind of kiss that consumed her.

It left her breathless.

Terrance watched Mona's lips move and couldn't resist tasting them. On impulse, he devoured her lips. When his tongue met hers she didn't protest but kissed him back with the same intensity.

He felt his heart skip a beat or two before his phone vibrated, interrupting the vibe between them. He pulled away, neither one acknowledging what had just occurred. He pulled out his phone. "It's my mom."

"You better answer it, or she'll be calling you all night," Mona said.

"You're right. And I don't need any unnecessary interruptions with what we have at stake."

"No, you don't," Mona agreed. She scooted over toward the window and looked out.

Terrance answered the call. "Hi, Mom. I'm on my way to a very important dinner engagement, so this will have to be quick."

"Why do I have a feeling you're trying to brush me off?" Sara asked.

"It's all in your mind, Mom. You know I talk to you at least once a day, so you're not going to make me feel guilty." He welcomed the phone call but wished it were from someone other than his mom.

He needed to figure out why he'd just kissed Mona. He kept his eye on her, but she wouldn't look in his direction. It was hard for him to gauge what mood she was in.

His mom talked on and on, but he barely heard a word she said. His mind was on two things: Mona and the network executives.

"Mom, we're almost there. I'll call you tomorrow morning, I promise."

Terrance ended the call without giving her time to say anything else.

"Mona, are you okay?" he asked as the car drove up the driveway of the luxurious hotel.

She glanced at him. "Yes, I'm fine."

"Great. Well, we're here. Let's show them what we got."

Terrance debated whether to discuss the kiss.

He chickened out. Mona said she was fine, so he believed her.

The driver opened the door. Terrance got out first and then assisted Mona out of the back of the limousine.

There were a few paparazzi outside. He placed his hand on the small of Mona's back. Bright lights from the flashing cameras nearly blinded them while they went inside the hotel.

Chapter Ten

MONA TRIED TO FORGET ABOUT the kiss but couldn't. She smiled when Terrance stopped and posed for pictures as they made their way into the hotel. Once inside, he introduced her to different people, acting as if they hadn't just shared a kiss. If he could forget the kiss, then she would have to try to do so also.

He led her to a table and pulled out a chair, and she took a seat. "I see someone I need to talk to. I'll be right back," he said.

As he left, Mona looked up to see Charlotte and Sean approaching the table.

"Mona, so glad you're here," Charlotte said.

Mona stood and hugged the couple before they all took their seats.

"Where's Terrance?" Charlotte asked.

"He's around here somewhere," Mona responded.

A waiter holding a tray filled with glasses of champagne asked, "Can I offer you anything to drink?"

Mona looked at the tray. "Sure."

The waiter left them with glasses of champagne. Mona got an extra one and set it in front of Terrance's spot.

"I'm so happy for you," Charlotte said.

"Nothing's happened yet," Mona replied.

"I'm confident yours will be the script they are interested in." Charlotte raised her flute. "To Mona and her script."

Sean held up his glass. "To Mona."

Mona smiled. Her attention was on Charlotte and Sean, so she wasn't aware that Terrance was nearby.

"To Mona," Terrance said as he sat beside her.

They clinked their glasses. Mona, who was normally cool and confident, felt a little uncomfortable. Terrance being so near made the room seem smaller. She felt herself perspiring. She picked up her napkin and wiped the sweat off her forehead and neck.

"Are you all right?" Charlotte asked. She must have noticed Mona's nervousness.

"I'm fine. I just need some air."

"Do you need me to take you home?" Terrance sounded concerned.

She shook her head. "No, I'll be fine. It's probably the champagne. The excitement. I'll be okay after I eat something."

Terrance said, "They're about to open the buffet line. I can get your food and bring you something back."

"I'm your assistant. Not the other way around."

"You've become more than my assistant."

Mona and Terrance's eyes locked, and neither looked away.

Charlotte cleared her throat. "Terrance and Sean, why don't you bring us both something back? I'll sit here and make sure Mona's all right."

A few minutes later, Charlotte and Mona were left by themselves. Charlotte said, "Spill it. What's going on between you two?"

"I don't know what you're talking about," Mona said. She picked up a glass of water and gulped it down.

"I can sense tension between you two, and it has nothing to do with work."

"Has Sean ever told you that you can be delusional?" Mona asked.

"Come on, don't be like that. Hurry before the guys get back."

Mona looked around. Terrance and Sean were standing in the buffet line holding two plates.

"We kissed on the ride here," she confessed.

"Are you serious? I was only joking about you two having something going on," Charlotte said.

"It was just a kiss. There's nothing going on between the two of us."

"Terrance is looking at you like Sean looks at me," Charlotte said.

"He and I shared a kiss, and that's all it was. Besides, I think I've met someone," Mona said.

"Who?"

She wasn't sure if she should share the fact that she'd met someone on the dating site. "His name is Falcon. He's a prominent businessman and he's everything I want in a man. So why would I chance being with Terrance when I've already met the perfect guy?"

"Well, I want to meet this Falcon if he's all that."

"You will, but after I do."

Charlotte shook her head. "What do you mean, after you do?"

Mona shared with Charlotte about 2-of-a-Kind. "Before you say anything, it was Kem's idea."

"I'm all for new-age dating. I hope it works out for you. But what I don't want you to do is turn down something real for a man you've never met."

"Terrance and I got caught up in the moment. I can guarantee you there will not be a repeat of what happened in the limousine earlier," Mona said, just as Terrance and Sean returned to the table holding plates of food.

Chapter Eleven

AFTER THEY ATE, CHARLOTTE SAID, "There's some people I want you two to meet."

Terrance asked Mona, "Are you up to it?"

Mona was reapplying her lipstick. "I'm fine. Thanks for being concerned."

Terrance got up and held her chair as she stood.

Charlotte said to Sean, "Baby, I'll be back."

Terrance placed his hand at the small of Mona's back when they walked, as if they were more than just colleagues. He noticed the glances Mona was getting in her emerald-green dress. He wanted to take off his jacket and cover her to stop some of the men's penetrating glares.

They stopped behind Charlotte, who said, "Charles, how are you?"

Charles gave Charlotte a hug. "I'm great. How are you, dear?"

"I wanted you to meet Terrance Beckham."

Charles extended his hand. "Terrance, I've heard so much about you. Can't wait to hear more about these ideas of yours."

Terrance shook his hand. "Mr. Osgood, I appreciate you giving me the opportunity to present. This is my co-producer, Mona Johnson."

Mona held her hand out. Charles took it and kissed the back of it. "A beautiful woman. You're a lucky man to have a woman like this by your side."

"We make a good team," Terrance responded. He didn't bother to correct Charles's way of thinking.

He noticed Mona frown, but then she smiled again.

"Charles, I know you have other people to see. I just wanted to formally introduce you two," Charlotte said.

"I look forward to seeing you all next week," Charles responded, right before walking away.

Terrance gave Charlotte a thumbs-up.

"My fiancé is trying to get my attention," she said. "So now that my job is done, I'll leave you two on your own."

"I'll call you tomorrow," Mona said. She faced Terrance. "I thought you would get a chance to pitch our ideas to him."

"No, that's not how it always works. Charlotte just wanted us to meet tonight. Monday, I'll present our material and hopefully walk away with a deal for us."

Terrance kept Mona near his side as he mingled with other people in various forms of entertainment.

"I appreciate you introducing me to your colleagues, but I'm a little beat," she said after a while. "I think I'm going to sit the rest of the night out."

"It *is* getting late. We can go."

"Don't rush on my account," Mona said.

"I've schmoozed enough. Come on, let's get out of here."

Terrance sent a text to the limousine driver. The driver was waiting for them outside at the curb.

Once they were inside the car, Mona removed her shoes. "Remind me not to wear shoes like this ever again."

Terrance laughed. "I don't see why women like to torture themselves."

"Because men like you love seeing us in these shoes."

"I can't deny that." He couldn't help but notice her toned legs. "Let me help relieve some of your discomfort."

Terrance reached for her foot and began massaging it. Mona leaned back in the seat. "Don't stop. That feels good."

The driver opened the partition. "Mr. Beckham, are you going to your house or the office?"

"Why don't you take us to my place? I'll drop Mona back at the office myself," Terrance said.

"Yes, sir," the driver said. He closed the partition.

Mona moved her foot. "Don't you think you should have checked with me to see if I had other plans?"

"I'm sorry. I should have. Do you? I can always have him get off at the next exit and take us to the office."

"No…I don't have any plans."

"I apologize for assuming you didn't have anything else to do. I'm just glad you feel comfortable enough for me to drive you home."

Mona rolled her eyes. "Please. I'm alone with you all of the time. Get over yourself."

"I just got *dissed*." Terrance pouted.

She laughed. "Please don't make that face again."

"Seriously, I can tell the driver to turn around." Terrance reached for the button to open the partition.

Mona placed her hand on top of his. "No. It's okay. I'll let you drop me off." She removed her hand and shifted closer to the door opposite where he sat.

Terrance didn't like small talk, but found himself doing just that as they rode to his house.

"I've always loved your house," Mona said as the driver pulled into the circular driveway.

"Thanks. I hate to say it, but my mom helped me pick it out."

"She does have good taste," she said, right as the driver opened the door.

Terrance helped Mona out of the limousine and tipped the driver generously. "Thanks, Mr. Beckham."

"That was sweet of you," Mona said as they walked toward the house.

"I know I can be demanding, but I'm really a nice guy," Terrance responded.

"I didn't say all of *that*." Mona laughed.

Terrance took his keys from his pocket and unlocked the door. He held it open and allowed Mona to enter first.

He closed his eyes as he inhaled the sweet fragrance of her hair as she walked in.

Chapter Twelve

MONA HAD BEEN TO TERRANCE'S house many times, so she wasn't a stranger to the layout. She'd always liked the spiral staircase and the chandeliers that hung above in the vaulted ceiling.

"Make yourself comfortable. I need to get something from upstairs, and then I'll be ready to go," Terrance said.

Mona went straight to the kitchen. She was thirsty and wanted a cold bottle of water. She flipped on the lights as she made her way down the long hallway. The walls were filled with framed movie posters and autographed photographs of different actors Terrance had worked with over the years.

She turned on the light, revealing a spotless kitchen filled with stainless-steel appliances. The yellow and gold decorative tiles and accessories brightened the room even more.

She opened the refrigerator and pulled out a cold bottle of water. She left the kitchen with the water in one hand and went to the living room. She stood in front of the fake fireplace and admired the pictures of Terrance in various stages of his life that sat in frames on the top shelf.

Mona was wondering what was taking Terrance so long. She glanced at the antique clock on the wall. It was almost ten o'clock.

That meant it would be near eleven before they made it back to the office.

She located the remote to the stereo and turned it on. The music blasted loud. Mona kept hitting the button on the remote until she decreased the volume. She hit skip until she got to a song she liked. The voice of Luther Vandross sang out through the speakers.

She swayed back and forth to the soft music.

"May I have this dance?" Terrance asked from behind her.

She turned around and saw his held-out hand. She took it and he pulled her close to him. She laid her head on his chest. She could hear his heartbeat, which mirrored her own. They slow-danced alone in his living room.

The song ended. Mona moved to pull away. She looked into Terrance's eyes. She felt hypnotized. Just like a magnet, their lips connected. She jolted when the electric current flowed from his body to hers.

Another slow song played in the background, but this time, their tongues danced to the rhythm.

Moans came out of both of their mouths.

"I want you," Terrance whispered.

Mona didn't want to think about tomorrow. Instead, she placed her arms around his neck and pulled his lips back on top of hers. Without stopping their kiss, Terrance used his hands and unzipped her dress. She slipped out of her dress, and it fell to the floor revealing her breasts and pink-laced panties.

He led Mona to the black leather sofa, got on his knees, and used one hand to push her panties to the side while devouring her with his warm and inviting mouth.

He flicked his tongue across her clit, causing her legs to tremble. Mona tried to steady herself. Terrance used both of his hands to hold her as he made love to her with his mouth.

Mona moaned. She'd never felt this much pleasure before. She wanted Terrance like she'd never wanted another man.

He stood and scooped her into his arms. He carried her up the winding stairway and into his master bedroom. She could have stopped him at any time, but she didn't. Her body trembled from the aftershocks of how he'd just made her feel.

He laid her on the thick black and brown comforter of his king-sized bed. She watched with eyes filled with desire as he undressed himself. He got on top of her, kissing her gently, while using one of his hands to remove her panties. His fingers dipped into her moist center, causing her to moan.

Terrance caught her moans in his mouth as he used his fingers to bring her to climax. She reached for him when he stopped briefly to retrieve a condom from the side of his bed. He opened the wrapper and, without saying a word, rolled it on his stiff, long member that stood straight out, needing attention.

Terrance took each one of her breasts in his hands, suckling and licking her nipples, causing Mona to beg for him to make love to her.

"I need to feel you inside of me," she moaned.

Terrance stared into Mona's eyes, lifted himself on top of her, and entered her. She closed her eyes and sighed with pleasure, wrapping her legs around Terrance's waist as he thrust in and out.

"Baby, you feel so good," he said.

Mona opened her eyes and gazed into Terrance's, which were filled with desire. His lips covered hers. Their moans got lost within each other's mouths. He elevated himself and gently raised her legs above her shoulders and re-entered her, causing Mona to scream out with pleasure. The sounds of the bed squeaking mixed with their moans filled the room.

They continued the naked dance as Terrance rocked Mona's world. They both cried out as they climaxed together.

Terrance fell on top of Mona. He squeezed her tight as if he didn't want to let her go. She held on for dear life. With their heartbeats in sync, Mona closed her eyes and drifted off to sleep feeling satisfied.

Chapter Thirteen

TERRANCE WATCHED MONA AS SHE slept. He didn't regret sleeping with her, but he didn't know what they were supposed to do after this. He'd been around plenty of beautiful women, so it wasn't just Mona's beauty that attracted him to her. Somehow, their spirits seemed to connect.

When he'd seen her enjoying the music, he was immediately drawn to her. All that night he'd felt more like her protector than her employer. He wanted other men to think they were a couple, so he'd made a point to not leave her alone.

He'd hoped they would get a chance to talk, but his sexual desires had overtaken his senses and he acted purely on those desires.

Terrance felt Mona stir. "Good morning, sunshine," he said.

She blinked a few times. "Good morning—I think."

"Being here with you makes it a good morning," Terrance said. He brushed her hair from off her face.

Mona sat straight up in bed, using the comforter to cover her nakedness. "Where are my clothes?"

"Downstairs. But you don't have to put those on. What's your size? I'll have someone deliver whatever you need."

"I have clothes at home," Mona said.

"Stop being stubborn."

"Now this is the man I'm used to. The bossy one," she said.

"Fine. Call me bossy. There's a new robe hanging behind the door in the bathroom. Everything you need is there. So what's your size, or do you want me to guess?"

"You've been around enough women, so figure it out," Mona teased.

She got out of the bed, dropping the comforter, allowing Terrance to see her full naked body in the daylight.

He wanted to reach out to her and pull her back in the bed. Instead, he watched her storm away into his master bathroom. She closed the door.

He put on the boxers on the floor on the side of the bed, then went downstairs and picked up her discarded dress. He looked at the tag and got the size off it, then called a boutique and placed an order.

He went back upstairs and heard the shower running. His first instinct was to join Mona, but he had second thoughts. Instead, he went to his huge walk-in closet and took a starched pair of jeans and a polo shirt off the hangers. He went to his dresser and got a pair of clean boxers and then went and used one of the other bathrooms.

After he showered, he dressed. He went back to his bedroom, but Mona was nowhere in sight.

He eased down the stairs and found her in the kitchen.

"Since I'm here, I thought I would cook us some breakfast," Mona said. "What do you want in your omelet?"

"Surprise me," Terrance said.

He liked seeing Mona in the kitchen. He wished the tie on the white robe would loosen so he could see her naked once more.

Mona caught him looking. "Last night was a one-night thing. I hope you savored the moment."

Terrance licked his lips. "It doesn't have to be. Maybe we should pursue this and see where else it leads."

Mona mixed the batter. "Business and pleasure usually don't mix well."

"There's always an exception." He moved closer to her.

"We're two grown folks, so what happened between us doesn't have to spoil our business relationship." Mona moved out of his way and poured the egg into a skillet.

"I don't know if I can forget about what happened last night so easily," Terrance confessed.

"T, you don't have a choice. Besides, I'm seeing someone."

"Who? When and where is this guy? Because I've never heard you mention a man." Terrance felt a little disappointed.

Mona stirred the omelet as she spoke. "I don't talk about my personal business with you, so you wouldn't know him."

"You come to all of my events. If I were your man, you wouldn't be attending them by yourself."

"Maybe he understands that I'm working and gives me my space."

"Maybe he's the wrong man for you, because if you were *my* woman, we would be spending as much time together as we could. Job or no job."

Mona sighed. "Truthfully, we haven't made a commitment, but I'm sure in time he will be asking me for one."

"If he hasn't asked for a commitment then that means you're fair game."

Mona held up the spatula. "Not to you, I'm not, Mr. Afraid of Commitment."

Terrance took a seat on the barstool at the counter and watched her cook. "I will commit to the right woman."

"So you're telling me out of all the women I've seen you with, not one of them were worthy of committing to?"

"No, I'm not saying that. But you know as well as I do that those women were only trying to get ahead in their careers. They weren't trying to get to know me on a deeper level."

"I agree with you. But it's your own fault. You wouldn't even know what to do with a woman of substance like myself, because you keep surrounding yourself with the shallow ones."

The doorbell rang.

"Saved by the bell," Terrance said.

They both laughed.

"You know I'm right," he heard her say as he left to answer the door.

Chapter Fourteen

MONA PLACED THE OMELETS ON two plates while Terrance went to answer the door. She hoped it was her clothes. The thick white terry-cloth robe covered her body, but she still felt naked around him.

She'd tried to pretend like what happened between them wasn't anything, but it meant more to her than she wanted to admit.

"Mom, let's go in the living room," she heard Terrance say. He was talking louder than normal, as if he were trying to warn her.

Mona didn't want his mom to see her in his kitchen wearing nothing but a robe. She had to think, and think fast. She opened one of the cabinets. If she held her stomach in, she might be able to fit inside. She tried, but the door wouldn't close.

Their voices were getting louder. Mona had two choices. She opted for the second. She ran out of the back door with nothing but a robe on. She could see Terrance's head from the window. She noticed him looking around, probably wondering where she was.

Fortunately, his house was far enough away from the next house that she didn't have to be concerned about a nosy neighbor. She turned when she heard a van. It parked behind Terrance's mom's Mercedes. When she saw the man park and get out of the van carrying a bag, she knew it was her clothes.

She ran out to him. The man seemed startled.

"Are you Mrs. Beckham?" he asked.

"Yes," she lied.

He handed her the bag along with a clipboard with a piece of paper on it and a pen attached. "I need for you to sign right here."

Mona signed the paper. The delivery guy stood there. She realized what he was waiting for. "I'm sorry, I left my money inside. I'm locked out. I'm glad you came with my clothes when you did. Can I borrow your phone?"

The delivery guy reluctantly handed her his phone. "I don't have much time."

"I promise you this won't take but a second." Mona dialed Terrance's number. He didn't answer. "Dang it," she said. She dialed again. This time he answered. "Terrance, don't hang up. It's Mona."

"Where are you?"

"I'm outside."

"What are you doing there?"

The delivery guy paced back and forth.

"Look, I have to give this guy back his phone. He dropped off some clothes. Is the front door unlocked?" Mona asked.

"It should be."

"Good. Keep your mom in the kitchen. I'll be in there shortly."

"Look, lady, I don't know what you got going on, but I need my phone. Don't worry about a tip."

Mona handed the deliveryman his phone and rushed inside of the house. She tiptoed up the stairs to Terrance's room and closed the door.

Terrance scratched his head, trying to figure out why Mona hadn't just slipped through the door that led up the back staircase instead of going outside.

In the meantime, he tried to figure out how to explain the two plates on the counter to his mom.

"I should have known you were entertaining some lady friend when I didn't get my early morning call," she said.

"Mom, it's only ten o'clock in the morning. I was going to call you."

"Well, I was out and in your area."

"You live at least an hour away."

"Okay, I admit I made a special trip. I do worry when I don't hear from you." She got a fork and started eating one of the omelets. "This is good. I guess those cooking lessons you took paid off."

"Mom, just eat the omelet and go. I have a busy day ahead of me. I was just about to get dressed and get out of here."

"I'll wait." She went to the refrigerator and pulled out a jug of orange juice, then went to the counter and poured herself a glass. She looked at him. "Do you want some?"

"No," Terrance responded. He threw his hands in the air when she went and took a seat at the counter.

"Dear, don't let me stop you from getting ready. I'll clean up when I finish. Aren't you going to eat your omelet?"

"I'm no longer hungry," he said.

"Pass it here. No sense in letting good food go to waste."

Terrance's mom was thin but had a healthy appetite. He handed her the plate, then left her alone in the kitchen to search for Mona.

She stood at the bottom of the stairway dressed in a pair of black fitted jeans that hugged her curves and a pink shirt.

"There you are," Terrance whispered.

"I need to get my stuff out of the living room," she whispered.

Terrance looked back. His mom was not behind them. They walked to the living room. Mona got her clothes off the couch. He picked the pillows off the floor and placed them on the couch.

They looked at each other and burst out laughing.

"I can't believe we're acting like teenagers hiding something from their parents," Mona said.

"I know. We're grown."

"Yes, so let's go tell your mom she's eating my breakfast."

"Uh… Let's not. Let me get rid of her. In the meantime, wait for me upstairs."

"But I thought we were grown," Mona teased.

"We are, but I don't feel like explaining things to my mom right now."

"I'm your assistant. She wouldn't think anything of my being here."

Mona didn't know Terrance's mom suspected her of being an opportunist. *He* knew Mona wasn't like the other women, but his mom didn't, and he wasn't going to add any ammunition to her suspicions.

Terrance walked Mona to the stairway. "Go," he said, shooing her away.

"Terrance, did I hear you talking to someone?" His mom's voice rang through the hallway.

Mona rushed up the stairs and into Terrance's room just as his mom got into clear view.

Terrance fumbled with his cell. "I was on the phone."

"Well, I've eaten as much as I could. I've let time get away from me. I have a meeting at the museum. You know, I could recommend you for a seat on the board."

"No, Mom. My schedule keeps me pretty busy as is."

"Well, you take care. And tell the woman you're hiding from me that if she's going to be a part of your life, she will need to meet me."

Terrance looked at his mother, stunned.

She kissed him on the cheek. "I'll call you later."

His mom walked out, leaving Terrance to his thoughts.

Chapter Fifteen

MONA AND TERRANCE LAUGHED THE majority of the way to the office as they reminisced about the events of the morning, leaving out their intimate moments. She wanted to discuss what had happened between the two of them but didn't know how to broach the topic. She'd hoped Terrance would bring it up, but since he didn't, she avoided it too.

He unlocked the office door. "I guess we can say this is casual Wednesday, since we're both in jeans."

"I guess so."

"Well, let me go work on this proposal. Once I finish, I'll definitely be asking for your input."

"No problem. I've got email and phone messages to go through myself," Mona said.

Terrance went to his office as Mona walked toward her desk.

There wasn't anything normal about this day, so she didn't go about her normal routine. If Terrance wanted coffee, he would have to ask for it or make it himself. She was still a little miffed that he hadn't acknowledged what happened between them.

She sat behind the computer and logged on. She checked her emails and saw that she had several from 2-of-a-Kind. She'd forgotten all about Falcon after the night she'd had with Terrance.

Her heart felt conflicted, because although Falcon seemed like he was perfect for her, she couldn't help how she was beginning to feel about Terrance. She clicked on the icon and sent a response to Falcon's message from the evening before. She must have logged off before getting that one.

She typed, *Falcon, I'm sorry I didn't get to respond last night. Something wonderful and unexpected happened.*

Mona began to go through her other emails until she heard a noise indicating she'd received a new message. She opened Falcon's response. It read, *I experienced something extraordinary last night myself.*

Something else we have in common.

Would you like to share your good news?

Mona looked at Terrance's closed door. *I got a promotion,* she typed.

That's great. What are you going to do to celebrate?

The only way to forget one man was to start talking to another one, Mona told herself. *I will be at the Flamingo Lounge later. Why don't you meet me there?*

Under the circumstances, I'm not sure it's a good idea.

She frowned. *If you change your mind, I'll be wearing a red dress with a red flower in my hair.* She hit the send button.

She continued to check her emails but didn't get another response from Falcon. The rest of the day went by with her and Terrance doing their best to avoid each other.

Eventually, Mona walked to Terrance's door and said, "T, if you don't mind, I'm going to call it quits."

He looked up from his desk. "Go ahead. I'll be all right."

"You sure? You've been in your office all day."

"I'm fine. I'll call you later," Terrance reassured her.

Mona was disappointed he still didn't address what had happened between them. Maybe it was easy for him to forget, but it wasn't easy for her.

She left the office and went home to change into her red dress and red heels. She fixed her hair and placed the red flower behind her right ear. She needed to forget Terrance, and tonight she would do that with or without meeting Falcon.

Terrance chatted with Raven off and on all day because he was trying to get what happened with Mona off his mind. He decided that after last night, he wanted to explore a relationship with Mona. His only issue was convincing her to do the same.

When Raven asked him to meet her, he declined. She seemed to be a nice woman, but she wasn't Mona. But Raven intrigued him, so against his better judgment, he decided to go to the Flamingo Lounge just to get a glimpse of the woman who'd captured his attention, if only briefly.

Terrance kept a change of clothes at his office because he never knew when he would have to go to a last-minute event, so he changed out of his jeans into a pair of brown slacks and a blue shirt. Less than an hour later, he was handing his keys to the valet at the Flamingo Lounge.

The popular lounge hadn't gotten crowded yet, so he was able to secure himself a seat at a table that gave him a clear view of the front entrance. He'd looked around and hadn't seen anyone in a red dress with a red flower in her hair. He ordered a glass of Remy Martin and people-watched.

He scanned the room again. He didn't know when he'd missed her grand entrance, but his eyes landed on the back of a woman in a red dress. His eyes traveled north, and that was when he noticed the red flower in her hair.

He didn't believe in coincidences, so he figured that he'd discovered the identity of Raven. He took a huge gulp of his drink. He needed it to calm his hormones. He was there to meet her, but he'd made up his mind that it wouldn't go any further than that. Terrance stood and walked in Raven's direction.

On the way there, he thought about what he would say. He didn't want her to think she'd wasted time chatting with him. He would explain to her that he hadn't expected to fall for a woman who was already in his life, that everything had happened suddenly.

Who was he fooling? The woman would laugh. She would think he was full of crap, because if he cared so much for this other woman, why would he be meeting her?

Before he could reach the bar, Raven turned around. Terrance's mouth dropped open. He stopped and contemplated what his next move should be.

Chapter Sixteen

MONA SIPPED ON THE APPLE martini the bartender had just handed her. One of the men at the other end of the bar paid for it. She smiled and mouthed, *Thank you,* then turned around holding her drink. The contemporary R&B music filled the room. Snatches of conversations could be heard throughout the lounge.

Mona got out her phone and checked to see if she had any messages from Falcon. She was a little disappointed that she hadn't heard anything since earlier. She took a seat on the barstool and nursed her drink.

"Hey, sunshine," a familiar voice said behind her.

Mona swiveled the seat around. "Terrance, what are you doing here?" He was so close, she could smell his woodsy cologne.

"I could ask you the same thing."

She looked around and then back at him. "I was supposed to be meeting someone, but I guess they aren't coming."

"Who? This mystery man you told me about?" he said, smiling.

Mona wanted to wipe the smirk off his face. "Maybe he's busy. Have you ever thought of that?"

"Ouch. You don't have to bite my head off."

"Don't make assumptions."

"Maybe he's not the one for you and it's best you find out now."

Mona couldn't agree more, but she wouldn't give up hope that Falcon would eventually show up. If he did, she didn't need to be in such close proximity with Terrance. She slid off the barstool.

"Office hours are between nine and five, Mr. Beckham. I'm off the clock, so if there's nothing else, I'm going to mingle."

"Have fun," Terrance said.

To her disappointment, he didn't follow her when she walked away.

A part of Terrance felt bad, knowing Mona was waiting for someone who would never show. He could have revealed his identity but felt it was best to keep the fact that he was Falcon to himself.

He would play along for now. He could probably use the Falcon character to his advantage. He just had to figure out how.

Terrance watched Mona from the bar. He'd drunk another glass of Remy Martin. He decided it would be his last, because he didn't want to get intoxicated and not be able to drive home. Plus, he needed to keep a watchful eye out on Mona.

He laughed to himself. It was funny that the woman he'd met on the internet was actually Mona. He thought back to the first time he met her. Mona's perky go-getter attitude was what made him decide to hire her.

From a distance, it appeared that Mona was in distress. He placed his glass on the counter and walked over to find out what was going on.

A man a few inches taller than Terrance stood near Mona. Terrance heard her ask the man to move. The man responded, "Why you got to be like that? I only asked you for a dance."

"My boyfriend's right behind you, and he's not going to like the fact you're trying to flirt with his woman."

The guy turned around and came face to face with Terrance.

"What's up, man?" Terrance asked.

"Do you know her?"

"As a matter of fact, I do. That's my lady, and I heard her tell you she wasn't interested." Terrance stuck his chest out.

"My bad. I'm not trying to start any trouble. She's looking fire in that dress, and all I was trying to do is get a dance. No harm, man."

"I'm here now, so I suggest you go find some other woman to bother."

The man held his hand up. "We good?"

"Just don't let it happen again."

The man dropped his hand and walked away. Terrance continued the charade. He walked over to Mona and placed his arm around her. "Are you all right?"

She nodded. "Thanks for coming to my rescue. He was a little aggressive."

"Why don't we get out of here? Have you eaten anything?"

"No, but I told you I was waiting for someone."

Terrance contemplated whether to tell Mona he was Falcon now. If he did, would she understand? Would she feel disappointed that it was him?

So many questions filled his mind. This feeling of insecurity was foreign to him. He didn't want to appear too vulnerable.

In the end, he decided not to take any chances. "You can always text him." Terrance knew she couldn't, because they hadn't exchanged numbers.

Mona seemed hesitant at first but then said, "Fine. Let's go. I am sort of hungry."

Terrance smiled. Mission accomplished.

Chapter Seventeen

MONA SAT ACROSS FROM TERRANCE in the diner located down the street from the Flamingo Lounge. When Terrance asked her to dinner, she'd originally assumed he was going to take her to a fancy restaurant, but instead, they were in a greasy diner. A place she never would have imagined Terrance at.

"After the night you've had, I think you could use a good, juicy burger," he said as he perused the menu in front of him.

"I am hungry. I've been eating junk food all day. I had plans for a good omelet, but we both know how that went."

They laughed at the memory of Terrance's mom showing up.

Mona took a few deep breaths as she got up the nerve to discuss the night they shared. "Terrance, about last night—"

Before she could finish, a server, wearing a name badge with "Bessie" on it, walked up to their table and screeched with excitement. "Hey, stranger! Hadn't seen you in a while." She placed two glasses of water in front of them.

Terrance responded, "I had to come by and see you. How are Jimmy and the kids?"

"Jimmy found him a new job. Pays more, but not enough for me to quit this gig. Besides, I'm still waiting on you to get me a part in one of your movies."

"Bessie, I haven't forgotten about you," Terrance said. "I want you to meet Mona. I was telling her about the burgers."

"T, she's as cute as a button. And small, too. She could definitely use one of our burgers. Sugar, what you want on yours? That one there gets the works." Bessie pointed at Terrance.

"Hold the pickles, onions, and mustard. Add cheese, please," Mona replied.

Bessie wrote that on her pad. "Got it. Two juicy burgers coming out soon. I'll throw a free dessert on there for you."

"Thanks, Bessie," Terrance said.

"I guess I should thank you again for coming to my rescue back at the Flamingo. Some dudes don't take rejection well," Mona said once Bessie had left.

"You're always rescuing me from my fiascos, so it felt good to return the favor." Terrance winked. His phone rang, and he glanced at it. "I need to take this call. I'll be right back." He slipped out of the booth and walked outside.

Mona looked around and saw that the diner was filled with people from all walks of life. Her stomach growled. She couldn't wait to get her food. She pulled out her phone and checked her social media while waiting for Terrance to return. She laughed at some of the funny memes.

Terrance slipped back into his seat. "What's so funny?"

"I was scrolling Instagram and saw this comedian I follow post a hilarious skit."

"I can get lost scrolling and laughing at those skits."

"Oh my goodness, yes." Mona laughed and gave her best reenactment of the joke.

Terrance laughed so hard he held his side.

"Here are your burgers. Enjoy," Bessie said, arriving with their food.

Mona took a bite out of her big, juicy burger. "Mmm," she moaned. In between bites, she said, "You're so right. This *is* good. Almost better than sex."

"The key word is *almost*," Terrance responded. He winked.

Mona squirmed in her seat. They continued to eat, but neither said a word.

Terrance paid the check and left Bessie a nice tip.

"I really hate for this night to end," he said while they walked to his car.

"I've enjoyed hanging out with you, too."

By now they were at the car. He held the door open. "The night doesn't have to end."

He leaned forward and, before Mona could respond, kissed her. She didn't pull away. Instead, she wrapped her arms around his neck. She forgot all about Falcon being a no-show. She also forgot about her original reservations over being with Terrance. She forgot about everything except the feel of his lips on hers.

She pulled back and used her fingers to wipe the red lipstick from his mouth. "Why don't you take me to my car, and then I'll follow you back to your place?"

"Now that's what I love to hear," he said.

Terrance drove her to her car and waited for her to get inside. She pulled off first, and he followed her down the highway.

The juicy burger had satisfied her taste buds, but only Terrance would be able to satisfy her sexual appetite. She kept trying to think of excuses why she shouldn't meet him at his place, but couldn't come up with any, so she didn't take a detour.

Mona parked in Terrance's circular driveway. He pulled in behind her, then walked to her door and held it open. She exited, and they walked hand in hand up the walkway to his front door.

Chapter Eighteen

THEY WERE BARELY INSIDE OF the house when Terrance and Mona began kissing. With lips locked, they removed each other's clothes.

Terrance had Mona pinned to the wall in the hallway. He cupped one of her breasts and flicked his tongue over her nipple. She leaned back on the wall and moaned. She wrapped her legs around Terrance's waist, and he held her buttocks in his hands. They kissed some more while he carried her in that position to one of the nearby guest bedrooms. He practically kicked the door in.

They fell on the bed. Terrance was on his back with Mona on top of him. She trailed kisses down Terrance's neck to his chest. When she reached his boxers, she reached into the opening and pulled out his erect penis and licked the head of it, catching him off guard. She wrapped her mouth around it as Terrance moaned in pleasure.

He placed his hand in her hair as she continued to pleasure him. She felt his penis enlarge in her mouth. She knew he was on the verge of exploding, so she stopped and eased on top of him and replaced her mouth with the wetness in between her legs.

"Monaaa," Terrance moaned over and over as she rode him like he were a stallion.

He placed one of her nipples in his mouth, causing Mona to get wetter and wetter as she bounced on him.

They held on to each other as Terrance erupted like a volcano inside of her.

He fell back on the bed, and she fell on his chest. Their heavy breathing eased into an even keel as they caught their breaths.

Terrance couldn't seem to get enough of Mona. They made love several times throughout the night.

The sunlight peeking through the curtains the next morning woke him. He reached for Mona, but she wasn't there. He noticed a note on the pillow next to him.

It read, *Your breakfast is in the microwave. I also put on a fresh pot of coffee.*

He hated that she'd left without waking him to say goodbye. After showering, he went downstairs. He picked up the discarded clothes that were now piled up outside of the guest bedroom. He removed his phone from one of the pockets. He'd received several calls, one from his mom, whom he would call later.

He called Mona's number as he placed the clothes in a dirty hamper. He got her voicemail. "Mona, baby, call me."

He disconnected the call. He wanted to hear her voice. Correction, he *needed* to hear her voice. He needed to know that everything was okay with her.

This was the second time they'd been intimate. Whatever was going on between them could no longer be avoided. He wasn't sure about her, but he didn't want to be with anyone else. Being with her was enough for him. She genuinely cared about people. It was an attribute that attracted him to her. He also liked the fact that whenever he needed her, she had his back. His life ran smoother with her around. Her feisty attitude also kept him in check.

He smiled as he thought of her, because most women were too busy trying to kiss up to him to be honest with him. Mona never backed down from telling him exactly how she felt.

He warmed up the omelet she'd made for him in the microwave. This time he was able to enjoy it. Then he went to his home office and started going over the television series proposal. The meeting with the executive was Monday, and he needed to make sure he was prepared. He didn't want to fumble during his pitch session.

Terrance threw his pen on the desk. He looked at his phone. He didn't have any missed calls. He dialed his cell number from the house phone. The cell rang, confirming he didn't have signal issues.

He called Mona again. This time she answered.

"I was just about to call you," she said.

"Thanks for the omelet, but it would have been better if we could have eaten breakfast together," Terrance said.

"I didn't want to overstay my welcome. Besides, it's Saturday, and I have chores to do, such as washing my clothes."

"Will I see you later?"

"Do you have something going on that you need my help with?"

Terrance tapped the pen on the table. "I sure do. I need to go over the pitch with you."

"Let me take care of my chores and then I'll be over. Let's say around four or five?"

"That works for me. I'll cook us something."

"You, cook?" Mona laughed. "I'm definitely coming over. I've never known you to cook anything."

"Just because you've never seen me cook, doesn't mean I can't."

"I'll be there with a hearty appetite, so make something good."

Terrance wasn't really a good cook, but now he had no choice but to deliver on what he'd promised. After hanging up, he called his friend, Chef Gavin. "Man, I need a huge favor. Can you come over and cook a meal for me? I need you to use my pots and pans so it'll look like *I* cooked."

"Oh, so which woman are you trying to impress? Is it the model, Moet? Or is it the actress I saw in your last movie, Paulette?"

"Gavin, I think I've found the one. But I just have to convince *her* that she's the one."

"Well, you don't want to start off under false pretenses. Why don't I come over? I'll tell you what to do, and if I see you need my help, I'll step in."

Gavin had a point. Terrance was already being deceitful by not telling Mona that he was Falcon. "Sounds good. Can you be over in about an hour?"

"Lucky for you, my schedule's wide open. But this will cost you. I'll stop by the market and you can pay me back later."

"I got you," Terrance said.

Later on that afternoon, Gavin coached Terrance in making a meal for two that he hoped Mona would enjoy.

Chapter Nineteen

CHARLOTTE AND KEM SAT ACROSS from Mona at the table in the coffee shop down the street from the gym.

"Doesn't sound like you need 2-of-a-Kind anymore. Things between you and Terrance seem to be heated," Kem said.

"That's just it. Is it about sex or more?" Mona asked. It was a question she'd wanted to ask Terrance but was afraid to hear the answer.

Charlotte sipped on her cafe au lait. "Didn't you say he wanted to pursue more with you? You're the one who's been hesitant."

"Ha. You're one to talk. Do I need to remind you how much grief you caused Sean before you finally gave him a chance?"

"This is not about me. This conversation is about you, so let's not change the subject," Charlotte said with a smile.

"People don't ever like talking about their own drama but want to be all in my business."

Kem laughed. "You're just as dramatic as some of my characters. I say give Terrance a chance. Forget the other dude."

"I'll think about it. For now, I'll enjoy our sexual escapades, but I want a man who is not afraid of commitment. If either one of you can tell me the last time you saw Terrance with the same woman twice, I will wash your car for the next three months."

Kem and Charlotte looked as if they were thinking. Neither said anything.

"My point exactly. I got other things to do. I'll see you ladies later," Mona said.

They hugged each other and then all went to their separate destinations.

Mona went home and took a long shower. After getting dressed, she decided to check in on the dating site one last time. There was still no message from Falcon.

She shrugged. *Guess he really was too good to be true.*

She put on her pair of black-and-pink sneakers that matched her jogging suit. She pulled her hair back into a ponytail and headed to Terrance's.

He greeted her with a hug and a kiss on the cheek when he opened the door. "Something sure does smell good," she said as she took in the aromas coming from the kitchen. Terrance was dressed in a pair of jeans and a polo shirt. "I guess I could have worn something else." Mona began to feel self-conscious.

"Nonsense. It's just the two of us. I thought we would eat and talk about the pitch afterward," he said. He led her to the dining room and held out a chair. "Have a seat."

Before she did, she asked, "Do you need me to help you with anything?"

"No. I will bring your plate out to you."

"I can get used to being served," Mona said as she took her seat. She sat near the end of the long oval dining table that could probably sit ten people.

It didn't take Terrance long to return. He brought in two plates with a silver covering. He placed one plate in front of her and the other next to her. "I have one more thing to bring out, and then we'll be ready to eat."

Mona took a peek at her food, lifting the silver covering. Steam from the food billowed out. She was impressed. The baked chicken with a white sauce looked tasty. The penne pasta and fresh green beans were a nice addition. He got an A for presentation.

Terrance walked in carrying a basket of buttered rolls.

"Don't tell me you cooked those from scratch?" Mona said.

He laughed. "No, you can find them in the frozen aisle. I did bake them in the oven. They're good. I've already tried one." He held out the basket.

Mona placed two rolls on her now-uncovered plate. Terrance said grace over their food, and they ate and talked in between bites.

"I have to say I'm impressed. The food was good. You should invite me over for dinner more often," Mona said. She wiped her mouth with her napkin.

"I'm glad you enjoyed it. It was definitely a labor of love." Terrance left out how he'd burned the first batch of sauce, because she didn't need to know that. With Gavin's help, he'd successfully made the sauce the second time around.

After they ate, Mona assisted him with cleaning the kitchen. They kept bumping into one another.

"I'm glad you have a dishwasher so I didn't have to wash everything by hand," she said.

"You've got something on your nose," Terrance said.

Mona wiped the top of her nose with the back of her hand. "Is it still there?"

"Yes, but now there's something on your mouth."

"Where are your paper towels?" she asked.

"Don't worry. I got it." Terrance covered her mouth with his.

Moans seeped out of Mona's lips. Terrance lifted her and placed her on the kitchen counter. The whirring of the dishwasher masked the sounds of their lovemaking.

Chapter Twenty

TO PROVE HIS COOKING SKILLS were no fluke, Terrance surprised Mona the next morning with breakfast in bed.

"You can cook bacon and toast. The eggs could have been fluffier, but you get a passing grade on breakfast too," she teased as she took her last bite.

Terrance's cell phone rang. He looked at the caller ID. "If I don't take this call, she's going to bug me all morning."

"While you take your call, I'm going to take me a shower."

Terrance answered his phone and watched Mona, wearing nothing but one of his t-shirts, walk to the bathroom.

"Terrance, do you hear me?" his mom asked from the other end of the phone.

"Yes. Loud and clear."

"Instead of lying in bed all day, you should be in somebody's church."

"Mom, I read my Bible. I do come at least once a month, so why are you complaining?"

"Look, boy, I don't have time to discuss this with you. Dinner's at four. The pastor will be there. Don't be late."

"About dinner… I'm not sure I will be able to make it. I have an important meeting tomorrow, and I really need to prepare for it."

"You are your father's son. Always with a million and one excuses."

"It isn't polite to talk ill of the dead, Mom. Isn't that what you've always told me?"

"Four o'clock. I'm not taking no for an answer."

Without another word, she hung up on him.

Terrance fell back on the bed and closed his eyes. He'd forgotten about his weekly Sunday dinner with his mom. All he wanted to do was stay in bed with Mona.

He could feel her presence before she said a word. He opened his eyes. She was fully dressed in the jogging suit she'd had on the night before.

"You and I need to talk," she said as she sat on the bed near him.

Terrance sat up straight. "We sure do. I need a date for dinner. Are you available?"

"That's just it, Terrance. We may be going a little too fast. We might need to slow things down just a little bit."

"Too late. Now that I've had a taste of you, there's no slowing down for me."

"But I told you I was talking to this other guy," Mona said.

"I thought after last night and the night before, this other guy would be the last person on your mind." Terrance felt disappointed that she seemed to care about this virtual stranger.

Mona eased closer to him. "The one thing this other guy can offer me that you haven't offered is a commitment."

"Did he show up the other night? No. So if he can't keep his appointments, how can he keep a commitment to you?"

"Technically, he never committed to meeting up with me."

"Have you heard from this dude?" Terrance knew the answer to it, but he wanted to hear her response.

"Uh. Well, no. But—"

"There you have it. It's been two days and you haven't heard from him. When men are interested in a woman, they will, number one, show up to meet you and, number two, communicate with you. Mona, I hate to sound cruel, but apparently your mystery man is just not that into you, so forget about the zero and focus on what's staring you straight in the face."

Mona frowned. "What? You haven't made your intentions clear."

"I want you. I want to see where this thing between us can go. I know we're attracted to each other, but I think it's about more than sex. I'm willing to give it a try, if you are."

"Terrance, there's no doubt you're a wonderful person. You can be a demanding boss, and you never date a woman long, yet I still think you're a good guy."

When she'd finished, he said, "I'm glad you think I'm a good guy, but you still have me pegged wrong. I am capable of committing to one woman."

"When was the last time you were in a committed relationship?"

Terrance groaned. "It's been a long time. Let's just leave it at that."

"See, my point exactly." Mona's hand went to his face. "Terrance, I like you. I really, *really* do. Being with you makes me forget about everything else. What I don't want to happen is for me to get so caught up in you that when you decide to move on to the next woman, I won't be able to function. I've had my heart broken too many times. I'm not looking to go back there, and besides, we're about to embark on this new TV show together. I've come too far in my career to let anything interfere."

He placed his hand over hers. "Whatever happens between us, I promise you, it will not interfere with our working relationship. I have no plans to ever hurt you. I care about you. The more time we spend together in this capacity, the more I'm drawn to you. Thoughts of being with another woman are the furthest thing from my mind."

"You say that now. But how will you feel next week? The week after that?"

"I can only hope that my feelings will grow. Mona, all you have to do is give us a chance."

"I'll think about it."

"While you're thinking, I have one other favor to ask you."

"What?"

"My mom wants me to meet her for dinner at four. Can you come with me? Her pastor is going to be there, and I have a feeling this might end up being an ambush. I need someone there to have my back."

"Only if you're paying me overtime, because dealing with your mama isn't part of my job description."

Terrance wrapped his arm around her. "But if we're going to be a couple, my mom will be in the picture."

Mona pouted. "I'm sure I'm not your mom's ideal woman for her son."

"She's happy as long as I'm happy," Terrance said, although Mona was correct in her assessment.

"I'll do it. But I need to go home and change into something more suitable. I wouldn't dare visit your mom dressed in this jogging suit."

"For the sake of time, why don't you order what you want from this boutique nearby and I'll have them deliver it here?" Terrance said.

"The benefits of having money. People like me can order online, but the quickest we can have it is the next day. Must be nice."

"It is nice when you can do it for someone you care about."

"Money can't buy my love, Mr. Terrance Beckham."

Mona kissed him on the lips.

Terrance couldn't be happier to hear her say that.

Chapter Twenty-One

BEFORE DINNER, MONA AND TERRANCE decided to go over the pitch for the show. She sat with her legs curled under her on the sofa. Terrance sat in the chair across from her and practiced his pitch. Overall, it sounded fine to her.

"Be sure to emphasize the sisters' bond. They may bicker among themselves, but they won't let others from the outside harm them."

"Gotcha. Maybe I should have you come along with me," Terrance said.

"I would be too nervous. I trust you to do a good job. It's your area of expertise, not mine."

Terrance looked at the clock. "Not sure of how much time you need to get dressed, but we should be leaving in the next hour to make it to my mom's on time."

"Thanks for the clothes. If I keep spending the night over here, I'm going to have a whole new wardrobe," Mona joked.

"You can change in one of the rooms near here, or you can use my bedroom."

"I'll use one of the guest rooms. I'll be back," Mona said, and left Terrance alone in the living room.

Mona was soon dressed. She wore a light-brown pantsuit with a white blouse. She opened the jewelry box and admired the faux pearls. They were beautiful. No one would know they were fake. She placed the earrings on, then went to locate Terrance.

He was in his bedroom, sitting on the edge of the bed, but looked up when she entered.

"You're looking dapper," Mona said. He wore brown slacks and a white button-down shirt and brown jacket with no tie.

"Thanks. You're looking beautiful, as usual."

Mona held out the pearl necklace. "Can you put this on me? I can't fasten it with this clasp."

He stood. "So you like the pearls?"

"Yes. No one should be able to tell they're fake."

He took the pearls from her hand. She held her hair as he placed them around her neck. "That's because they aren't."

Mona removed her hand and let her hair fall back into place. "I will return these as soon as we get back from your mom's."

They were now face to face. "You will do no such thing. I bought them for you. They're yours."

"I can't accept it. You've already bought me far too much stuff."

"Look at it as a bonus for being such a great assistant," Terrance said as he walked to the dresser and retrieved his car keys. "I'm ready if you are."

"Sure," Mona responded.

Terrance didn't know what to say to prepare Mona for his mom. They listened to music the majority of the one-hour drive to Pasadena. When they got close to his childhood neighborhood, he began sharing some of his history with her.

"You would think the way my mom acts that we always had money, but that's not the case. My father moved us here after becoming vice president of operations at this local plant. He also made some wise decisions when it came to the stock market. He owned shares of Amazon during its early years, and it made him a very wealthy man."

"I rarely hear you speak of your dad. How long ago did he die?"

"Five years ago, from a heart attack. He was golfing, so he went out doing something he loved."

"Your mom's probably a little clingy because she's missing your dad."

Terrance disagreed. "My dad explained it to me when I was a teen. Apparently I had a little brother that died before I was born. My mom blamed herself for his death because she had him on the bed and left the room for a few minutes, and when she'd returned, a pillow had fallen on top of him and smothered him to death."

Mona gasped. "I'm so sorry. I know it must have been devastating to her."

"I just wish I could figure out a way to get her out of my business without hurting her feelings."

Mona reached over the center console and placed her hand on top of his. "You'll find a way."

"You don't mention your family. Why is that?" Terrance said.

"You never asked."

"I guess I've been so busy being busy that I never took the time to get to know you on a personal level. So tell me about them now."

"Fortunately for me, we live in different states. My folks are both alive and well and live in Frisco, Texas, which is in the suburbs of Dallas. My older sister and brother are married with kids. The grandchildren seem to occupy my parents' time, so that keeps them from always trying to get in my business."

Terrance wanted to learn more about her family, but by now they were in the driveway. "Don't be nervous," he told her.

"I wasn't nervous until you said don't be nervous." Mona flipped down the visor and reapplied her lipstick in the mirror.

"My mom has hired help too, so just wanted to warn you," Terrance said before slipping out of the driver's seat to open Mona's door. "After you, my lady."

Chapter Twenty-Two

MONA ADMIRED THE BEAUTIFUL MEDITERRANEAN-STYLE house as she followed Terrance up the stairs leading to the front door.

A woman dressed in black greeted them. "Terrance, so glad to see you, son."

Mona had seen Terrance's mom before, but this woman didn't look like her. She looked to be in her sixties, with gray streaks in her hair, which was pinned in a bun.

Terrance hugged her. "Gilda, this is Mona. Mona, this woman helped raise me. She's like my second mom."

Mona extended her hand. Gilda pulled her into an embrace instead. "It's about time Terrance brought a woman home to meet us."

"Oh, no, it's not like that. We work together."

"My eyes don't deceive me," Gilda said.

Mona blushed. "This is a nice home you have here."

"Thanks. But I'm just the help. The mistress of the house is waiting for you both in the parlor."

"Gilda, you are more than the help and you know it," Terrance said.

"Tell that to your mama. Let me get the food on the table so I won't have to hear her complaints."

"Gilda's the cook-slash-housekeeper and, when I was younger, also my nanny," Terrance informed Mona while they walked inside.

Mona couldn't help but notice the expensive-looking paintings on the wall and the extravagant chandeliers hanging above them as they walked down the grand hallway.

"Are you ready?" Terrance asked while standing outside of a door. He placed his hand on the doorknob.

Mona took a deep breath and plastered a smile on her face.

Terrance opened the door.

Sara Beckham stood about five feet, five inches. The brown-skinned older woman didn't have a wrinkle on her face. Her sandy-brown hair was free of any gray strands thanks to hair dye. She wore a navy-blue designer dress with pearls adorning her neck, and several diamond rings covered her fingers. She greeted Terrance with a hug and kiss on the cheek.

"Mom, you remember Mona." Terrance moved to the side.

"Mona, yes. The young lady who works for you." Sara looked Mona up and down.

Mona extended her hand. Sara touched the tip of her fingers and shook it.

A gray-haired man wearing a black suit stood behind Sara. He was almost the same height as Terrance.

"This is Reverend William Hamilton," Sara said.

Mona noticed how Sara's voice seemed to soften when she spoke his name. Mona and Terrance shook the pastor's hand.

Gilda walked into the doorway and said, "Dinner's ready."

"You two can wash your hands in there," Sara said, pointing. "Terrance, show her where the bathroom is. Come on, William. We'll meet them in the dining room."

A few minutes later, they were all seated at the table. Reverend Hamilton said grace over the food.

They were served roast beef, mashed potatoes, green peas, and rice pilaf with rolls.

"Terrance, I wasn't aware you were bringing a guest," Sara said. "But thankfully, Gilda always makes extra."

"Mom, you act like Mona being here is an intrusion."

"Your words, not mine." Sara looked away.

Reverend Hamilton said, "Now, Sara, what did I preach about today?"

"Terrance knows I don't like surprises," she responded.

Mona rolled her eyes. Something told her that even if Sara had known she was coming with Terrance, she wouldn't have approved.

"Mona, so you're working weekends now?" Sara asked with a scowl on her face.

"I don't have a typical nine-to-five job. There may be times where I'm with Terrance for days on end. It just depends on what he wants."

Mona smiled. Terrance gave her a funny look.

"You're a beautiful woman, in a peculiar sort of way. You should be dating instead of spending so much time with my son."

"Your son is all the man I need right now."

"William, please excuse her. These young people today have no respect for their elders or men of the cloth."

"Reverend Hamilton, I meant no disrespect," Mona said.

"None taken," the pastor said. "Sara, eat your food. It's getting cold."

But it wasn't as cold as the look Sara gave Mona.

Terrance didn't like how rude his mother was being to Mona. He would address it as soon as they were alone.

Reverend Hamilton turned to him. "Terrance, I've known you since you were a little boy."

"Yes, sir."

"I respected your dad and have always had the utmost respect for your mom. Sara thought it would be best for me to be here when she shared some news with you."

Terrance stopped eating. He held his breath. He'd lost his dad. As much as his mom could get on his nerves, he didn't want to lose her too.

Sara said, "William, let's finish dinner first."

"No. I think it's time now."

Terrance looked at Mona, and she looked away. "Mom, out with it. The suspense is killing me."

"Well, dear." Sara looked at William and then across the table at Terrance. "The reverend, I mean William, has asked me to marry him."

Terrance laughed. It was a joke. His mom and the reverend? He looked at each of them, shook his head, and laughed again.

"Dear, I'm serious. I wanted you to be the first to know. Didn't know we would have company, but oh well."

Terrance had had no idea his mom was interested in remarrying after his father died. This news came as a shock. The reverend wasn't just his pastor; he was one of his father's friends. To Terrance, this was a betrayal.

He pulled away from the table and left the room without saying a word.

Chapter Twenty-Three

MONA WATCHED THE SCENE PLAY out. She looked at Sara and asked, "Aren't you going to go check on him?"

"Terrance is just throwing a tantrum. He'll be all right."

"Terrance is a thirty-two-year-old man. He's far from being a child."

Sara looked at Mona with fiery brown eyes. "I don't need you to tell me anything about my son."

"Apparently you do. Can't you see what you told him upset him? Instead of trying to be bitchy with me, you should be going to console your son."

"William, are you going to let this woman come into my house and disrespect me?" Sara shouted.

Mona stood. "I'm going to find Terrance." She walked out while Sara complained to the pastor about what she deemed rude behavior.

Mona looked from room to room until she found Terrance. He was standing in a room, staring at a big portrait hanging on the wall. The painting looked like an older version of him.

Mona stood close and looped her fingers through his. "He's handsome."

"That was my dad."

"You look just like him."

"That's what I've heard all my life."

"Your mom… I'm sure she's been lonely without your dad."

Terrance turned and faced her. "You just don't understand. The reverend was my dad's friend. How could he try to get with his friend's wife?"

"Not sure of the dynamics of the relationship, but T, your dad's gone. Your mom is still a woman. If the reverend makes her happy, then why not be happy for her?"

"But…" Terrance trailed off.

"Don't you *want* her to be happy?" Mona asked.

"Yes, I do."

"Problem solved. Your mom doesn't need your blessing, but it would be nice if you gave it to her." Mona squeezed his hand.

Terrance looked into her eyes. "You're a wonderful woman. My mom was rude to you, yet you're being the voice of reason in this mess."

"We can talk about that another time. Right now, you and your mom need to talk."

Sara walked into the room.

"I'll be in the dining room if you need me," Mona said. She released Terrance's hand and walked away.

Sara frowned at her when she walked by.

"Next time, leave the hired help at home," Sara said as she walked closer to Terrance.

"Mona is her name, and she's more than the hired help."

"I don't like her. She has no class."

"If you're going to continue to insult my guest, then I can leave." Terrance headed toward the door.

Sara grabbed his arm. "Son, don't. We need to discuss my engagement."

He jerked his arm away. "If you were so concerned about my input, you would have talked to me *before* you accepted the good reverend's proposal."

"William's a good guy. Don't be like that."

"He's taking Dad's leftovers. Now that's a stand-up man for you."

"Terrance, I want you to be happy for me. You don't know how lonely I've been since Freddie died. When he died, a part of me died with him. I thought I could never experience happiness again. William's been there with me every step of the way. We didn't set out to fall in love—it just happened."

Terrance could see the sincerity in his mom's eyes. He didn't want to argue with her. Like Mona had said, his mother was grown. She really didn't need his permission. "But don't you think it's kind of weird to be with your husband's friend?"

Sara laughed. "Yes. But your dad's no longer here. I'm free to date who I please."

"Please spare me the details. If you want to marry him, I won't stand in your way."

She hugged him. "Thank you, baby. I knew you would come around."

"Don't thank me. You should be thanking Mona. She helped me realize you deserved a second chance of happiness."

"I guess she's not all bad."

"No, Mom. She's not bad at all." Terrance hugged her again. "Love you."

"Love you too," Sara said, squeezing Terrance tight.

Chapter Twenty-Four

THREE HOURS LATER, MONA WAS sitting on her couch in her apartment. After they left Terrance's mom's place, she'd decided to go home instead of hanging out with Terrance. She needed time alone to think about a lot of things. She'd explained to Terrance that she needed to do some things to get ready for the coming week.

She wasn't hungry but wanted some banana fudge ice cream. She threw on a jogging suit and drove to the corner store.

She was in the process of getting back in her car when she heard someone call her name.

"Mona, is that you?" a familiar male voice said.

"Garrett?" Mona couldn't believe that the man who'd broken her heart so many years ago was standing right in front of her.

"I'm so glad I ran into you. There's so much I need to tell you. Can I get your number so I can call you later?"

"I think you said it all nine years ago." Mona didn't wait for him to respond. She jumped in her car and sped away.

She saw Garrett running behind the car in her rearview mirror. How dare he think she would want to speak to him after he broke her heart? She thought about what happened nine years ago.

He hadn't had the courage to break up with her himself, so instead he had his mom do it.

Hours later, Mona tossed and turned in her bed as she dreamed of Garrett and relived the breakup over and over. She woke up the next morning feeling as if she hadn't slept in days. She noticed she had several missed calls from Terrance.

Mona glanced at her puffy eyes in the mirror. She slipped on a pair of sunglasses and headed to work.

Terrance hadn't slept well the night before. He kept dreaming about his father. He wished Mona had stayed and spent the night. His mom called him right before he got to the office, but he decided he wouldn't talk to her until after his meeting with the network executives. He blocked out his personal issues and concentrated fully on the job.

He heard a buzzing sound, indicating someone was coming through the door. He yelled, "Mona, is that you?"

"Yes, boss, it's me," she responded.

He perked up at the sound of her voice. He got up from his desk and went to greet her.

She placed her purse and keys on her desk and looked at him. "You're here bright and early."

"Today is the day, or have you forgotten?" Terrance asked.

"Of course not." She took a seat behind her desk.

"Oh, I don't get a kiss, or at least a hug?" Terrance teased.

Mona put a finger out in front of her and moved it from one side to the other. "Not in the office."

He pouted. "Just one little peck. Please?"

"I'm only doing this because you have that meeting." She walked around her desk and placed her arms around Terrance's waist.

He didn't wait any longer, and kissed her with an intensity that rendered them both breathless. Terrance's hand roamed over Mona's body. He felt himself getting aroused, so he stopped.

"Now I can go to the meeting with confidence," he said with a huge smile on his face.

"Give me a minute to catch my breath," Mona responded, a huge smile on her face as well.

"Are you sure you don't want to come with me? I could use your support."

"I think me being there would be a distraction."

"I disagree."

Mona ignored his comment. "I heard your pitch. It's perfect. You've done this type of thing before and I haven't. Maybe once I get some experience, I'll feel more at ease about doing it."

"You have to start somewhere."

"Terrance, I appreciate you having confidence in me, but this is too important to take any unnecessary chances. You got this. I'll be here when you get back." Mona kissed him lightly on the lips and then took a seat.

Chapter Twenty-Five

TERRANCE LEFT THE OFFICE EARLY just in case he ran into traffic. He would rather be early than late. Charlotte's assistant Felicia had already called to make sure he hadn't forgotten about the meeting.

Terrance couldn't seem to get Mona off his mind as he weaved in and out of traffic. His lips still tingled from the kiss they'd shared earlier. He smiled thinking about how she made him feel.

His thoughts were interrupted by the sound of the horn coming from behind him.

"Oops," Terrance said. The light had turned green and he was still sitting there.

Less than an hour later, Terrance was seated in the reception area waiting for Charlotte.

He heard her before he saw her. She seemed to know everyone working in the office. He heard her greeting different people as she made her way around the corner.

"Hi, Terrance. I'm sorry I'm a little late." Charlotte extended her hand, revealing freshly manicured nails and a huge, sparkling engagement ring.

"I'm just glad you're here. I'm normally not this nervous."

"Let me do the negotiating. You just concentrate on the stories. I got the rest," Charlotte assured him.

Terrance sighed with relief. "I wish Mona would have come."

"I spoke with her while on the drive over. She's confident that you will represent her story well."

He smiled. "Has she told you anything else?" He knew how close Mona and Charlotte were, so he was curious to know if Charlotte knew the extent of their relationship.

Charlotte smiled. "I like you, Terrance. You have great ideas. You love your community and it looks like you love my friend—but for now, we'll table this discussion."

Before Terrance could respond, a woman in a vibrant emerald Pink Lucy jumpsuit walked over to them.

Terrance stood.

"They are ready for you now," the woman said.

"Great," Charlotte responded.

Terrance followed the two women toward an office surrounded by glass. He noticed that there were ten people seated around a conference table before he walked through the door.

Charlotte slowed and said to him right before going in, "Don't be nervous. You've got this."

Terrance hoped so.

They entered the room and introductions were made. Charles Osgood, the man he'd met at the dinner party, led the meeting. "Terrance, we were just discussing how excited we are to be working with you. We've allotted the next two hours, so the floor is yours."

Although he'd pitched show ideas before, it didn't erase the nervousness he felt. Terrance said a silent prayer, which gave him the confidence he needed. He walked to the front of the room with all eyes on him as he pitched the two story ideas.

Mona kept checking to make sure her phone was working. She wondered how things were going with Terrance. Did the network executives like his ideas? Did they specifically like hers?

She was going through the normal Monday morning routine of checking emails and returning messages when the door opened. Mona saw a delivery guy holding a huge bouquet of flowers. "Is Mona Johnson here?" he asked.

"I'm Mona."

"These are for you. Can you sign this to confirm delivery?" He handed her the colorful bouquet.

Mona moved things around on her desk with one hand while holding the bouquet with the other. She placed it on her desk.

The delivery guy held out a form. Mona signed. She reached into her desk drawer and pulled out some money from her purse to tip him.

Once the delivery guy was gone, she removed the card from the plastic stick to read it.

She read out loud. "'These flowers are beautiful, but not as beautiful as you. Thank you for being a ray of sunshine.'"

She smiled when she saw Terrance's name written at the bottom. She wanted to call him but wasn't sure if he was still in the meeting.

The door opened again. The delivery guy returned, this time with a bouquet of red roses.

"I just realized I had another delivery for you," he said.

Mona stood and took the roses. "These are beautiful."

"Is it your birthday?" he asked.

"No. But I love flowers, so I'm not going to complain." Mona took the vase of red roses and placed them on the other side of her desk.

The delivery guy cleared his throat. Mona looked at him with a "what" look on her face. She'd given him a nice tip the first time. It wasn't her fault that he'd had to return a second time. Her tip for him was, "Thank you. I hope you have a good day."

He stood there for a few seconds and then left.

"That's what I thought," Mona said.

Terrance is really pouring it on thick, she thought when she located the card attached to the vase. But the flowers were from Charlotte and Kem.

Mona smiled and sat behind the computer. She sent the girls a quick text to thank them for the roses. She was about to call Terrance to thank him for the flowers he'd sent, when her cell rang.

"Mona, it's Garrett."

"How did you get my number?" she asked.

"Your sister gave it to me."

"My *sister*? I can't believe it. I'm going to kill her."

"Don't be mad at her. She understands my need to see you. Please, give me the opportunity to speak with you in person," Garrett said.

"I probably shouldn't, but there are a few questions that I want to ask you. Questions I deserve answers to."

"Great. When can we meet?" he asked.

"Not sure. How long will you be in L.A.?"

"I'm here for good. You're one of the reasons why I've come back."

"Garrett, you can save the BS for another woman. You fooled me once. I'm not falling for it again."

"I don't want to argue with you. Once you hear me out, you will sing a different tune."

"I doubt it. I got your number on my phone. I'll call you and let you know when I'm available to meet. When we do, it will be in a public place. Is that understood?" Mona asked.

"Of course. We'll meet at a place of your choosing. Thank you for giving me an opportunity to make things right," Garrett said.

"Yeah, whatever. I'll call you." Feeling a little frazzled, Mona disconnected the call before Garrett could respond.

Chapter Twenty-Six

TERRANCE BIT HIS BOTTOM LIP while sitting out in reception. Charlotte said to him, "This is good. If they weren't interested, they would have sent you home. Trust me. I've been to many of these types of meetings."

"I hope so. I love doing movies, but to have my own show on television… It would be a dream come true."

"It's going to happen." Charlotte looked at her vibrating phone. "I need to take this. I'll be right over there." She stood and walked out of hearing distance.

Terrance took his phone from his pocket and turned it on. He'd received messages from his mom and other people, but there weren't any from Mona. He sent her a text message. A few seconds later, she responded.

He smiled. She loved the flowers. He'd ordered them online right before leaving the office. She sent him another text message inquiring about the meeting. He typed: *It's promising. We're waiting to be called back in.*

The same woman from before walked up to him. "They are ready for you."

"Thanks," Terrance responded. He sent Mona a message to let her know he was about to go into another meeting.

Charlotte's back was toward him. He tapped her on the shoulder. Startled, she jumped before turning around.

"I hate to interrupt, but they're asking for us," he said.

Charlotte ended her call and they walked to the conference room. This time there were only two people in the room, Charles and another man. Charlotte and Terrance took seats directly across from them.

Charles extended his hand across the table toward Terrance. "Terrance, welcome to the company. We're excited to have you on board."

Terrance shook Charles's hand. He then shook the other guy's hand.

"Which pitch will you be going with?" Charlotte asked.

"We have two slots available, but my team was really interested in the one about the sisters, so we want to develop that one. And this here is David Anderson. He's from legal. We just need you to sign a few papers."

David handed Terrance a single sheet of paper and held on to what looked like a thick document. Terrance placed the paper in between him and Charlotte. He read it, then looked at her for guidance.

"Terrance will sign this one so you'll know that he is serious and will not pitch this idea to any other network during our negotiation phase—however, we will need our legal team to read over the full contract before he'll sign the other agreement."

"Sure. That's understandable," David said. He handed Charlotte the full agreement.

Terrance signed the single sheet and handed it to David. Charles and David signed, then David said, "I'll be right back with your copy."

Thirty minutes later, Terrance and Charlotte were in the parking lot walking toward their cars. "Do you want to tell Mona or do you want me to?" she asked.

"Let me. I will tell her in person because I want to see the expression on her face."

"I have a suggestion. Do you think you can wait until later? Let's surprise her. I'll have her meet me at our favorite restaurant. We can have a celebration dinner."

"Sounds like a good idea to me. It's going to be hard to keep it to myself, but let's do it," Terrance replied.

Mona stared at the flowers on her desk. It was sweet of Terrance and her friends to do this for her. The *ding* indicating someone was coming to the door interrupted her thoughts.

There stood Terrance with a huge grin on his face.

"How's my favorite person?" he asked. He walked to her desk and smelled the colorful floral arrangement.

"They smell good, don't they?" she asked.

"What's *that*? I didn't order you roses. Are those from that mystery guy of yours?" Terrance asked, a curious look on his face.

"No. They're from Charlotte and Kem."

"The ladies are making me regret not ordering the roses." He smiled.

"I love the floral arrangement. You did good," she assured him. Mona attempted to get off the subject of flowers. "So, what happened? Any news?"

"None right now."

Mona's phone beeped. It was a message from Charlotte. She read it and looked at Terrance, who was still smiling.

"You have a few calls you need to return." Mona handed him a long yellow sheet of paper.

"I'll take care of these. If you want to leave early, you have my permission."

"Only if you're going to pay me for the full day."

"You got it, sunshine."

"You don't have to tell me twice. I have some things I need to take care of anyway, so I'll see you tomorrow." Mona removed her purse from the desk drawer.

"Tomorrow. What about tonight?" Terrance asked.

"Maybe. I'll let you know." She stood and gave him a quick peck on the lips.

Mona needed to take care of old, unfinished business, and tonight was the night.

Chapter Twenty-Seven

MONA LEFT THE OFFICE AND made an emergency trip to the hairdresser. She wanted her hair to look *fierce* when she saw Garrett. She knew she shouldn't care, but she wanted to look so good when Garrett saw her that he would regret ending things with her.

While sitting under the dryer, she received a text from Charlotte asking her to meet her at Luigi's Restaurant at eight. Things were falling into place. She wanted to meet Garrett in a public place, so Luigi's would be perfect. If she met him at seven, it would give them an hour to talk, and then she could send him on his merry way.

She waited until she was sitting in her car to call Garrett.

"I didn't think you were going to call me back," he confessed.

"Unlike you, I'm a woman of my word. You have one hour. Meet me at Luigi's at seven."

"An hour's all I need. See you then, beautiful."

This time, Garrett ended the call first.

Later, Mona found herself changing in and out of outfits. Her bed was covered with clothes until she finally decided on a black pencil skirt with a lilac blouse and short black jacket that matched the skirt.

She draped a towel around her so she wouldn't get anything on her outfit while she applied her makeup. Satisfied with her appearance, Mona left to meet Garrett.

The restaurant was busy with patrons. The hostess asked, "Are you waiting for someone?"

"I'm supposed to be meeting a man named Garrett."

"Are you Mona?" she asked.

"Yes."

"He's here. He wanted us to bring you to the table once you arrived. Follow me."

Mona followed the hostess. She could see the back of Garrett's head and felt her heartbeat increase the closer they got to the table.

The hostess said, "Mr. Garrett, your guest is here."

Garrett, all six feet and two inches of him, stood. Although he wore a designer suit, Mona could tell he was muscular.

"It's so good to see you." He reached out to hug her, but Mona moved out of his way.

"I wish I could say the same to you."

He cleared his throat, then pulled out her chair. "At least let me hold out your seat."

Mona tried to keep the old emotions at bay. The turmoil within her wouldn't allow her to let her guard down around him.

She remained quiet as she listened to Garrett fill her in on what he'd been doing for the last nine years. He'd made many strides in the area of medicine. He'd recently moved back to Los Angeles and opened a private practice. He'd become the doctor he'd always wanted to be. He'd followed his dreams and lived a fulfilling life, from what he said, and all without her.

"So what's been going on with you?" he asked. "And you could have ordered something other than a salad."

Mona stopped eating and looked directly into his eyes. "I'm a grown woman and will eat what I want. I don't need for you or anyone else to dictate what I eat."

"I'm sorry. I was just saying. I'm not trying to control you. I've never tried to control you."

"No, because you always let your mother do that for you," Mona snapped.

Garrett placed his fork on his plate. "That's what I really wanted to talk about. My mom did some things that she shouldn't have."

Mona sat back and looked at him. "Does it look like I care about that now?"

Garrett looked at her hands. "I see you don't have a ring on your finger. So maybe I still have a chance?"

She laughed and then stopped abruptly. "A snowman has a better chance of not melting in a fire than you have of getting back with me."

"Just hear me out, please. I'm sure you'll change your mind."

Mona glanced at her watch. She needed Garrett gone before Charlotte and Kem got here. "You're wasting time. Say what you have to say so we can go our separate ways."

Garrett blurted, "I had no idea my mom was the reason why you gave me back my ring. She just shared that with me a few months ago. I've been trying to get in touch with you ever since."

"I gave her back the ring because you sent her to break up with me. You were a coward and didn't have the decency to do it yourself."

"Listen, Mona. Please. I never wanted to break things off with you. In fact, I loved you, and my intention was to marry you. My mom was supposed to tell you I had to leave to go out of town for an interview with Johns Hopkins Hospital, not end our relationship."

Mona was confused. She recalled the day it had happened. Garrett's mom knocked on her apartment door. She walked in with a smug look on her face, looked at Mona as if she were nothing, and said, "Garrett's moving to Maryland. He wanted me to tell you, and he also wanted me to tell you he no longer wants to marry you. I'm sorry to be so blunt, but it's best you find out now."

After hearing those hurtful words, Mona had felt like she had no choice but to give him back the ring. She removed the engagement ring from her finger and placed it in the woman's extended hand. Garrett's mom left without another word, leaving Mona alone to deal with her broken heart.

"Mona, did you hear me?" Garrett asked.

She snapped back into the present. Tears formed in the corners of her eyes, but she refused to cry.

"So you didn't break up with me? This was all your mother's doing."

"Yes, that's what I'm trying to tell you. I wanted to marry you. I *expected* to marry you. After my interview, I flew back to L.A. My mom met me at the airport. She handed me the ring I'd given you and told me the bad news, that you'd broken off our engagement. I didn't want to believe her. When I went to your apartment, your roommate told me you'd moved."

"I was devastated. I went to stay with Charlotte. She and Kem watched over me until I had the strength to move on."

"I'm so sorry. I'm here because I want to make things right with you. Just give me the chance." Garrett reached across the table and placed his hand on top of Mona's.

She sat stunned. The pain from years before dissipated in the air with this revelation. He had actually loved her as much as she'd loved him.

Chapter Twenty-Eight

TERRANCE MET CHARLOTTE, SEAN, AND Kem outside of the restaurant. They all walked inside together. The hostess led them to their reserved table.

Kem said, "That looks like Mona there."

They continued to walk toward their table. Terrance got a clear view. It *was* Mona, and she wasn't alone. That explained why she hadn't returned his calls or text messages.

Mona looked past her male guest and right at Terrance. It was no secret to Charlotte and Kem that Terrance and Mona were involved.

"Come on. She knows we're supposed to be here. She'll find us," Charlotte said.

"Y'all go ahead. I'll be there in a second," Terrance responded.

He refused to go sit with Charlotte and the others until he found out the identity of the man sitting with Mona. He made a beeline to her table.

Mona stammered, "T-Terrance, what are you doing here?"

"I should be asking you that question."

Terrance never took his eyes off the man sitting across from Mona. The man introduced himself without waiting for Mona. "I'm Garrett, Mona's fiancé."

"Fiancé?"

"He means *ex*-fiancé," Mona said.

"Well, don't let me interrupt your cozy dinner," Terrance said, feeling repulsed. Mona had never revealed to him that she'd been seeing someone, other than the fictitious guy she met on the internet.

He walked away, leaving Mona alone with her ex-fiancé, or whoever he was, and went to sit with Charlotte and the others. Tonight was supposed to be a celebration for them all, but he didn't feel like celebrating.

"Was that Mona?" Kem asked.

"Yes. It was her," Terrance snapped.

Mona came to the table and said, "Hi, everyone." She looked at Terrance. "May I speak with you in private?"

All eyes were on him. Terrance didn't want to cause a scene, so he pushed away from the table. Without saying a word, he headed out the front door, Mona walking behind him.

When they stood outside the restaurant, Mona blurted, "What you saw isn't what it looked like."

"You two looked mighty cozy to me, but you know what, I don't even know why I care. It's not like you've made a commitment to me."

"I want to," Mona said.

He laughed. "Are you serious right now?"

"Terrance, stop tripping. That guy is someone from my past. There's nothing going on between us. You've got to believe me."

Kem walked outside. "I came to make sure you two were okay."

Mona said, "Garrett called. I met him here because I knew we had plans for dinner."

"Jackass Garrett, the one who broke your heart back in college?" Kem asked.

"Yes, one and the same."

Kem said, "Terrance, trust me. You don't have to worry about Mona getting back with Garrett. I'm not sure what all she's told you, but I was there. Their breakup almost broke Mona. I'm going to leave you two to finish talking. We'll just order appetizers until you come back." She hugged Mona and left them alone.

"So is Kem right?" Terrance asked.

"Yes. Garrett's my past. I want you." Mona grabbed his hand.

"What were you doing here, talking to him? Things looked real intense from where I stood."

"Let's get through dinner and I promise you I will tell you everything later," Mona replied.

Terrance wanted to know now, but agreed to wait. "Let's go back in. No need to keep everyone waiting."

When they neared the table, Charlotte said, "There they are. The two people we are here to honor."

Terrance held Mona's seat out for her. "What is she talking about?" she asked him.

He retrieved a glass of champagne from the table and turned to her. "Mona, the reason why Charlotte wanted you to meet them here for dinner is so we could celebrate our new TV show."

"What do you mean by *we*?" she asked.

"The network wants me to produce your show about the sisters."

"Oh my goodness!" Mona exclaimed. Her hand shook so much she had to put her glass down. "I've been dreaming of this moment forever. Thank you, Terrance."

She wrapped her arms around his neck and kissed him, almost causing him to drop his glass.

Everyone around the table congratulated them. They drank champagne, ate food, and talked over the next two hours. Terrance smiled and was happy to see Mona happy—but he wouldn't be completely at ease until he knew the story behind her ex.

Chapter Twenty-Nine

MONA GOT IN HER CAR and followed Terrance home from the restaurant. Her phone rang. She used the button on the steering wheel to answer.

"I'm staying at the Omni. Please stop by so we can finish our conversation," Garrett said.

"I've moved on. I suggest you do the same." Mona felt bad for Garrett, but she couldn't go backward.

"I tried to move on, but none of those women were you. I've never stopped loving you."

Mona felt conflicted. "If you'd come back into my life earlier, then maybe, but now it's too late."

"I'm not going to give up on you. On us," Garrett stated.

Another incoming call came in. She saw Charlotte's number on the display. "I need to take this call. Have a good life." Mona clicked over. "Hey, Char."

"What were you doing there with Garrett? Are you trying to sabotage your relationship with Terrance?" Charlotte blurted.

"Terrance and I are not in a relationship. We are just sleeping together."

"Mona, I know you. I know you wouldn't be sleeping with Terrance unless you had feelings for him."

"It's called lust."

"Lust and love, but back to Garrett. What's going on with him?"

Mona shared with Charlotte what Garrett had revealed to her. "So can you see my dilemma?"

Charlotte remained quiet.

"Are you there?" Mona asked.

"Yes. Just gathering my thoughts. That's a lot to lay on a person."

"How do you think *I* feel? Terrance walked over to the table just a few minutes after Garrett told me this."

"You *did* let Garrett know you were seeing someone, didn't you?" Charlotte asked.

"Yes, but Terrance and I aren't, like, in a committed relationship."

"Can't tell that from the way he acted when he saw you sitting at the table with another man. I could see the steam coming from his head when he marched to your table. I told Sean he might need to intervene."

"Terrance actually had a lot of self-control. I don't know if I would have been that calm if I saw him with another woman."

"I suggest that you make it clear to Terrance that Garrett isn't a threat to what you two have."

"I will. But can you believe it? Garrett didn't end things after all—his mom did."

"Terrance is your destiny. Garrett's your past. Now don't forget that," Charlotte said, right before ending the call.

Mona parked her car behind Terrance's. He walked over and opened the door for her, then they walked in silence inside his home.

"Would you like anything to drink?" he asked, once inside.

"No, I'm fine," Mona responded.

"Make yourself at home," Terrance said. "I need to go check on something."

She slipped off her shoes and walked through the hallway to the living room, placing the shoes by the sofa. She located the remote to the stereo and found an R&B station to listen to.

Terrance walked around the coffee table and took a seat next to her on the sofa. He raised her leg and began massaging her feet.

"So tell me about this dude," he said, getting straight to the point.

Mona leaned her head back while enjoying the massage. "Me and Garrett were college sweethearts. By now we should have been married with two-point-five kids and a white picket fence."

She opened her eyes. Terrance wasn't laughing. "So what happened?" he asked.

Mona shared with him her version of what happened. "But I found out tonight that some of what I knew was based on a lie." She went on to share with him the new information.

Terrance looked shocked. "Wow. How vindictive. She must have really hated her son to do that to him, and to you."

"I was never good enough for her son, who was destined to be a doctor," Mona conceded.

"I'm sorry for what she did to you all, but that was then. This is now. I love you, and I don't want to lose you to some man from your past."

Mona opened her mouth to speak but stopped. Had she just heard what she thought she heard? "Terrance, tonight's been filled with a lot of excitement. I want to make sure I heard you correctly."

Terrance moved her leg, got closer, and planted kisses all over her face. "I love you."

"I love you too, Terrance." Mona's eyes watered.

He removed her blouse and cupped her breasts. He slid one breast from underneath her bra and took her nipple into his mouth. He repeated the same thing with the other. Mona moaned in pleasure.

"Let's take this to the bedroom so I can make love to you the way I want to," Terrance said in a low, husky voice.

Mona held on to his hand and followed him.

Chapter Thirty

TERRANCE AND MONA WERE NOW naked on top of the covers. He lay on his back as she climbed on top of him, straddled him. She leaned forward and kissed him while rotating her hips. Terrance caught each one of her moans with his mouth.

Mona fell back as Terrance tilted his head forward and brought her left nipple into his mouth. She increased the pace. Terrance could feel her muscles tightening around him.

"Terraaance," she moaned.

He felt her leg shaking, stopped suckling on her breast, and eased Mona off him, gently rolling her onto her back. He used one hand to open her legs, felt the moisture in between her thighs. He looked into her eyes and, without saying a word, penetrated her.

He cried out, "Mona, ooh, baby."

Their eyes locked. She wrapped her legs around his waist as he thrust in and out. Terrance moaned. Mona moaned.

He bent over, and their lips locked as he pumped in and out of her, causing them both to climax at the same time.

Terrance collapsed on top of Mona and then to the side of her, wrapping his arm around her waist. He was in total bliss.

"Mona, did you mean what you said back at the restaurant?"

She shifted closer to him. "What, baby?"

"You said you wanted a commitment."

"Yes, but only if you want one," she replied.

"Mona, I wouldn't have confessed my love for you if I didn't want a commitment."

She moved around until they were facing each other. "Terrance, don't play with me."

He kissed her forehead. "I, Terrance Beckham, agree that I will date Mona *exclusively*."

"Then it's official. We are a couple."

"Yes, you're mine and I'm all yours," Terrance teased.

They made love again and afterward fell asleep in each other's arms.

The sound of Terrance's alarm clock the next morning woke them.

"Ugh, I really wish we could stay in bed all day," Mona said.

"Me too, baby, but we can't. There's so much to do. I have a meeting with my attorney about the contract, and I need you to work on scheduling and suggestions for actors." Terrance sat on the edge of the bed.

Mona leaned on her side. "I'm going to be a little late. I have to go home, shower, and change clothes."

"Let me walk you out. I'm meeting with the attorneys, and then I'll see you at the office."

After they dressed, Terrance walked Mona to the front door. He wrapped his arm around her waist and kissed her. Neither seemed to want to let go.

Mona left Terrance's place feeling like she was on cloud nine. After a quick shower and getting dressed, she was back in her car. With music from one of her favorite playlists playing, she made it to work without feeling rushed.

She was singing along to a Chaka Khan song at her desk when she heard the chirp of the door.

"What are you doing here?" Mona asked when she came face to face with Garrett.

"You didn't return any of my calls. I thought I would try you at work."

"Look, Garrett, coming here wasn't a good idea."

"But I thought after our conversation last night that you would see things a little differently."

"I'm sorry your mom tried to ruin our lives, but I'm over it. I'm happy now."

"But Mona, please. I can't lose you a second time." Garrett's eyes were filled with tears.

Mona couldn't help but feel compassion for him. She walked over and gave him a hug. He held her tight. When she started to pull away, he attempted to kiss her, but she turned her face and his kiss landed on her cheek.

She pushed his arms away and walked to her desk. "Garrett, my boss will be here any time, and I really don't think you being here is a good idea."

"I never thought you would be the type to sleep with your boss to get ahead," Garrett snapped.

"*Excuse* me?" Mona placed a hand on her hip.

"I googled your boss. He's the same man you're seeing. Mona, he may be able to offer you the glitz and the glamour, but he can't give you the type of love you deserve. Remember how we used to stay up all night talking, laughing, and sharing our dreams?"

"Do you remember how much your mom despised me? How she hated me so much she lied and tried to ruin our lives?"

"But my mom's no longer a problem. I'm older. I'm wiser. I'm my own man. My mom doesn't make my decisions for me anymore."

Mona clapped. "Good for *you*."

"This guy, your boss. If you're worried about losing your job, I have an opening for a receptionist; you can work for me."

Mona laughed. "Around here, I'm more than just a receptionist. In fact, you're looking at a professional screenwriter. One of my stories will be a sitcom."

"Congratulations. See, we're both living our dreams. I'm a doctor. You're a screenwriter. Baby, this is our time."

Mona held her hand in the air. "Our time has passed, so bye-bye."

"I'll leave for now. But I will be back."

"Bye, Garrett."

He walked out the door and almost ran into Sara.

Ugh, just what I need, Mona thought.

Terrance's mom walked in with a smug look on her face. "Oh my, did I interrupt something?"

"No, you didn't," Mona responded. "If you're looking for your son, he's out of the office until later. I'll be sure to tell him you stopped by."

Sara stood near Mona's desk. "You might have my son fooled, but I see right through you. You're an opportunist."

"Mrs. Beckham, you don't know anything about me."

"Whatever, missy. Tell my son to call me." She stormed out of the door, leaving Mona alone.

Chapter Thirty-One

"MOM, CALM DOWN," TERRANCE SAID while weaving in and out of traffic as he drove toward his office.

"Your office is a place of business, not a place for her to entertain her men," Sara proclaimed from the other end of the phone.

Terrance had just left his lawyer's office. Prior to his mom's call, all was well in his world. His career was taking off in a new direction. Mona, the woman he'd fallen in love with, had agreed to date him exclusively. He was happy.

Terrance hurriedly parked and walked briskly into the office. Mona looked at him when he entered.

"Hey. How did things go?" she asked in a bubbly voice.

"The lawyers made a few changes. Once they agree, we can sign and everything will be official. But what's this I hear about a man being in my office?"

"No hug. No kiss. No nothing?" Mona pouted.

He gave her a quick peck on the lips. "Now back to my question."

Mona turned to her computer screen and started typing. "Your mother needs to mind her own business. It was nothing. Just an irritating salesman trying to sell something, and I wasn't buying it."

"Are you sure? Because the way she made it sound, it seemed like it was personal."

She stopped typing and looked at him. "We need to get something straight. In order for things to work out between us, I need for you to not allow your mother to interfere in our relationship. Do I need to remind you of what happened with Garrett and how that turned out?"

"I'm not your ex, so don't ever compare me to him—or any other man, for that matter."

Terrance stormed away, went to his office, and slammed his door. He paced back and forth in front of his desk until he calmed down.

He removed his jacket and swung it on the chair.

"Your mom's on the phone," Mona said over the intercom.

"Tell her I'll call her back," Terrance replied.

A few seconds later, there was a knock on the door. Mona entered without waiting for him to respond. By now, he was seated behind his desk.

Mona stood in the doorway. "I know you're upset, but you will not talk to me in that tone of voice."

Terrance's emotions were getting the best of him. After last night, some of his insecurities were coming to the surface, and he had to admit that his mom had played a role in his attitude.

"I'm sorry, okay? Things just got tense. I didn't know what was going on. I blew things out of proportion, and for that, I'm sorry."

"Look, Terrance, I can understand your frustrations. But we just confessed our love for one another last night. There's no way I would jeopardize our relationship."

Terrance's frown turned into a smile. "I'm relieved. Come here." Mona walked over, and he pulled her onto his lap. "You're making me go crazy. I see now why it's taken me so long to commit to someone. All of these new emotions I'm feeling. Seeing you with your ex last night almost drove me crazy, and then my mom saying some man was here…"

Mona laughed. "I'm not like those other women you're used to dating. When I'm committed, I'm committed. I'm yours, so you have nothing to worry about."

She kissed Terrance to reassure him of her dedication to him just as his cell phone vibrated. "Ugh. Let me see who this is and get rid of them."

Mona stood and straightened out her skirt. "I need to finish some items on my to-do list so I can get the list of potential actors to you. You take care of your call and I'll get back to work."

Terrance answered the phone and watched Mona sway her hips while walking out of the room.

"Sean, I'm surprised to hear from you," he said.

"Charlotte gave me your number. I was a little concerned after seeing you so upset last night. We're going to be in the same circle, so I thought I would reach out and check on a brother."

"I appreciate it. I'm fine. Mona and I worked out our differences. I got a little jealous but found out I really didn't have anything to be jealous about."

"Look, if you want to hang out or just talk, give me a call," Sean said.

"Sure, man," Terrance said.

After the call, he went through his messages. He read the press release Charlotte's secretary had sent over and responded with his approval. Then he looked at the photo of his father sitting on his desk. "Dad, I wish you were here. Your little boy is about to get his own TV show. Can you believe it?"

Chapter Thirty-Two

MONA LEFT THE OFFICE WITH plans to meet Terrance later at his place. She felt guilty about not coming clean about Garrett's appearance in the office earlier. She probably would have told him if his mother hadn't made it sound like she'd walked in on them in a compromising position. Mona wondered how long Sara had been standing there. Had she seen the hug? Had she seen Mona's tears as she officially closed the door on her past?

Terrance's attitude had struck a nerve with Mona, so she'd gone into defense mode. After learning that Garrett's mother had lied and changed the course of her life, Mona refused to deal with another meddling mother.

She parked her car outside of Terrance's house. This time she'd brought an overnight bag so she could go directly from his house to the office the next morning.

She rang the doorbell. Terrance held his cell phone to his ear with one hand and opened the door with the other. He greeted her with a hug and quick peck on the lips. He used his available hand and grabbed her carry-on bag.

He whispered, "I'll be off in a minute."

The aroma of the spaghetti sauce from the kitchen filled the air. Mona watched Terrance walk up the stairway with her bag. She turned and went to the kitchen. She walked to the stove and removed the top from a boiler to reveal spaghetti and meatballs simmering.

The buzzer on the oven went off. She placed an oven mitt on and opened the door. She removed the pan of garlic bread and put it on top of the stove.

Terrance walked in and turned off the burners on the stove. "Thanks for getting that for me. Have you checked the messages at the office? Charlotte informed me that the press release went out. She's gotten a lot of interview requests."

"No. Not since earlier. I'll go check now."

"Let's eat, and then you can get to work on it."

"Yes, sir." Mona saluted him.

"I'm sorry. I didn't mean to sound demanding."

"I'm your assistant too, so I'm not tripping."

"We need to talk about making some changes, but we can do it later."

After dinner and cleaning the kitchen, they headed to Terrance's home office. Mona sat behind the computer. "What's your password?"

Terrance recited his password. Mona logged on to her work email and read out loud some of the interview requests.

"I'll do all of those. I'll let you handle my schedule. Just don't overbook," Terrance said.

"Turn your printer on for me, please," Mona said.

Terrance turned the printer on and Mona printed out the emails.

Mona stood and removed the pages from the printer. Terrance walked behind her and placed his arm around her waist. "This can wait until tomorrow."

"Business before pleasure," Mona said. "I don't want anyone to accuse me of slacking on my job because I'm sleeping with the boss."

"We're a two-man machine, so no one cares."

"Your mom does." Mona pulled away from Terrance. She went and sat back behind the desk.

"My mom doesn't run my business," he assured her.

"Does she know that?"

Terrance's cell phone rang. "Her ears must be burning, because it's her now."

"You go talk to your mother, and I'll work on this."

"Hi, Mom," Terrance answered. "No, I've already eaten." He took a seat in a chair across from the desk.

While he talked with his mom, Mona went back to working. She set the papers out in front of her and looked at the calendar on her phone. She began making notes on the paper.

Terrance looked uncomfortable. He kept moving around in his seat. The frown on his face showed that he wasn't too happy about how the conversation with his mom was going. Mona decided at that point to eavesdrop.

"Mom, we've gone over this before. I don't need you interfering in my personal life."

Mona wondered what Sara was saying.

Terrance ended the phone call. Mona asked, "Does your mom know about us?"

"She suspects something is going on, but no, she doesn't know that you and I are in a relationship," he admitted.

"Why haven't you told her? It's cool if you don't, but I'm just curious."

"It's none of her business."

"True, it's not, but if we're going to be in a relationship, I don't see why our liaison has to be some secret."

"Mona, baby, I have no problems with our relationship being made public."

"My friends know we're together, so that's not what I'm talking about. I don't want our relationship to be a secret from your mom because you're afraid to do something you think she might not approve of."

Terrance leaned forward and stared her straight in the eye. "I'm not your ex. I will not let my mother interfere with what we have going on. My mom doesn't speak for me. Unless you hear it coming from my mouth, don't concern yourself with what she says."

Chapter Thirty-Three

TERRANCE, WEARING A BLACK BROOKS Brothers lapel suit, tapped his foot while standing at the end of the stairway. He glanced at his Rolex. He needed Mona to hurry, because he didn't want to hear his mom complain if they were late to her engagement party. He'd decided that he would reveal that Mona was more than just his assistant at the party.

"Mona, don't mean to rush you, but we need to go, dear," he yelled from the bottom of the stairway.

"I'm coming," Mona responded.

She seemed to glide down the stairs in her four-inch Jimmy Choo crystallized suede and mesh sandals. Terrance smiled. He'd known when he saw the Tracy Reese black and metallic cross-pleated skirt that she would look good in it.

Terrance held his arm out, and she held on to it as she stepped off the last stair. "You look beautiful," he said.

"Thank you. You're looking quite dapper yourself," Mona responded.

"Our chariot awaits."

Terrance opened the front door. Mona's mouth opened in surprise. "We're going in style, I see."

"Yes. Since my mom wanted to throw a grand affair to announce her engagement, I thought, why not?"

A little over an hour later, the limousine pulled into the circular driveway. The driver went past the expensive cars parked and stopped near the front of the stairs leading to the Beckham house.

Terrance and Mona exited the limousine and walked behind others inside. They were greeted by servers holding trays of hors d'oeuvres as soon as they entered. Soft music from a live jazz band filled the house.

Terrance knew his mom had a thing for throwing elaborate parties, but he hadn't been expecting to see this many people. He greeted several people he knew and introduced Mona to them as they made their way through the house.

He heard his mother's laughter before he laid eyes on her. She stood next to another woman looking regal in an Oscar de la Renta ivory-and-black cocktail dress.

Sara looked at Terrance and motioned for him to come closer to her.

"There's Mom," he said, leading Mona toward his mother.

Sara gave him a tight hug. "How's my baby?"

"I'm doing fine."

He watched his mom give Mona a once-over. "You look nice," she said to Mona. Then she looked at Terrance. "What is she doing here?"

"She's my date." He grabbed Mona by the hand. She squeezed it.

"Date?" Sara said.

"Yes, Mom. Date. Mona and I are seeing each other. We're a couple."

Sara shook her head. "There are too many people here now. We'll address this issue later."

"There's nothing to discuss. I'm with Mona. Deal with it."

Sara grabbed a glass of champagne from a nearby waiter and gulped it down, and then returned the empty glass to the tray.

Reverend Hamilton walked over and placed his arm around Sara's waist. "Hi, Terrance—and Mona, isn't it?" he asked.

"Yes. Nice to see you again," Mona responded.

"I think there are enough people here for me to make my toast. Come on, Terrance. I want you up front too." Reverend Hamilton led Sara to the front of the living room. She kept looking back at Terrance and Mona, who walked behind them. Instead of smiling, she looked upset. Terrance looked at Mona but wasn't able to read her. Her facial expression remained neutral.

Terrance wanted to do something that he hoped would ease the tension. "Reverend Hamilton, let me make the announcement." He hoped with this gesture, his mom would tone down her open disdain toward Mona.

Reverend Hamilton walked over to the band, and they stopped playing. He handed the microphone to Terrance.

"Listen, everyone," Terrance called. People turned to face them. The noise level decreased. "It is my pleasure to announce the reason why you're all gathered here tonight. On behalf of Reverend William Hamilton and my mom, Sara Beckham, we would like to thank you for sharing in this momentous occasion with us. My dad loved my mom, and I believe in my heart that he would want her to move on and find happiness with someone else. So it is with a clear heart and conscience that I would like to be the first person to officially congratulate my mom and Reverend Hamilton on their engagement."

Tears flowed down Sara's face as the crowd yelled out congratulatory comments. Terrance hugged his mom. He reached out to give Reverend Hamilton a hug, and the pastor pulled him into a brotherly embrace. "Thank you, son, for your blessing."

Terrance moved out of the way as different people congratulated the couple.

"You did well," Mona said from beside him.

"I hope she's happy." Terrance looked at his mother, whose face was covered by a huge smile as she hugged well-wishers. He noticed many admiring her huge engagement ring.

"You took the high road. I admire you for it," Mona added.

Terrance gave her a quick peck on the lips. He caught a glimpse of Sara looking at him, and her smile faded into a frown. The only thing he could do at that point was shake his head.

Chapter Thirty-Four

MONA WANTED TO LEAVE THE engagement party but remained because of Terrance. She knew when she wasn't wanted, and Sara had no issue making that known. If she wasn't making snide comments, her evil glare when she looked her way made Mona want to smack her, and of course she couldn't do that.

Mona kept her composure even when it was obvious that Sara was trying to humiliate her. Terrance tried to be a buffer between the two of them.

"Mona, I'm so sorry. I promise to talk to my mom later on," he said to her as they stood away from the crowd of people near the band.

He walked over to the leader of the band and whispered in his ear. The band started playing another song. Terrance grabbed Mona by the hand. "Come on. Dance with me."

She looked around. "No one else is dancing."

"So? You said you knew how to step, so let me see if you really do." Terrance smiled.

Mona enjoyed a challenge. She'd learned how to step from her relatives in Chicago. She and Terrance used the small, open space and began dancing. Mona was finally starting to enjoy herself.

They were gaining a small audience. Some of the people watching decided to join in, and the area they were in expanded into an official dance floor.

Terrance pulled Mona close to him. "See, now aren't you glad I talked you into dancing with me?"

She leaned back and smiled. "Now *this* is a party."

"Yes, it is." He swirled her around and then dipped her.

After they'd danced for the next hour, Terrance led her off the dance floor.

"I'm thirsty," Mona said.

"Wait right here. I'll go find us something to drink." He kissed her on the cheek and left in search for drinks.

Mona stood and swayed to the music.

"Look who I ran into," Sara said from behind her.

Mona turned around, and her mouth dropped open when she saw Sara's arm looped through Garrett's.

"Garrett is here with my good friend, Dr. Carson," Sara said with a smug look on her face.

"Hi, Mona," Garrett said.

Mona's mouth went dry. She couldn't open it to say anything.

"When I saw Garrett, there was something so familiar about him, and then it dawned on me how I knew this handsome doctor. He's the man that I saw leaving my son's office. Knowing that you two knew each other, I had to come make this introduction." Sara removed her arm from Garrett's. She moved past Mona and said, "Terrance, do you know Dr. Garrett?"

Mona looked and saw the frown on the returning Terrance's face. She could see how intense he was from the way his forehead wrinkled.

"We've met," Terrance responded.

His mom took one of the glasses he held. "Thanks, dear. My throat is a little dry." She took a sip. "I met Garrett the other day at your office. Well, I didn't know he was a doctor then."

He looked directly at Mona when he asked, "Is this the guy who was the 'salesman'?"

Mona knew she'd been caught in a lie. "Terrance, let me explain."

Sara eased to the side and smiled.

Mona reached for Terrance's arm, but he jerked it away. "Why did you lie to me? I asked you about it, and you told me it was a pesty salesman."

"It was nothing, that's why," Mona said.

"It was something," Garrett interjected.

Mona and Terrance said in unison, "Shut up," and then turned back at each other.

"This is enough," Sara said. "You're drawing attention to yourselves. Dear, now you see Mona's just like I said she was, so it's best that you find out now and cut your losses."

Mona clenched her fists by her sides, or else she feared she would punch Sara in the face. She waited for Terrance to correct his mom, but he just stood there. Her blood pressure increased. "Aren't you going to say something?"

"What? What do you expect me to say?" he asked coldly.

"Fine. I'm not going to stand here and be insulted. I'm out of here."

Mona rushed passed some gawkers. Terrance didn't follow. She got outside, and that was when it dawned on her that she didn't have her car. She turned to walk back in, but Garrett was right on her heels, so she bumped into him.

"I'm parked over there if you need a ride," he said.

Mona didn't want to ask Terrance for anything, so against her better judgment she responded, "Sure. I'll take you up on your offer."

Chapter Thirty-Five

TERRANCE HAD ALLOWED HIS EGO to get in the way of common sense. He should have followed her.

"Let her go, son," Sara said.

"No. Mona's right. Mom, she's important to me, so you will not insult her if you want me to come around."

"You're taking her side over mine." Sara's smile faded.

"No. I'm just trying to do what's right, and that means I should be going after Mona instead of standing here talking to you. I need to make this right."

Without waiting for his mother to respond, Terrance rushed out the front door and down the stairs looking for Mona. He looked around and saw other people getting in their cars. The light of a black Maybach caught his attention. On the passenger side was Mona, and Garrett was the driver.

Terrance's head fell because he'd just lost his woman to her past. He'd handed Mona to Garrett on a platter. "Damn…damn… damn," he said, not caring who was around him.

He didn't bother to go back inside the house. He didn't want to face his mother. He walked to the limousine. The driver said, "Mr.

Beckham, I saw your guest leaving, but she'd left her purse in the car so I tracked her down and gave it to her."

"Thank you," Terrance whispered.

The driver opened the back door and Terrance got inside. Frustration, anger, and disappointment set in. He popped the cork off one of the bottles on the bar and poured himself a drink. He placed the glass on the little table and drank directly from the bottle.

By the time the driver got to his house, Terrance had drunk the entire bottle. Mona's car was parked outside. He opened the front door and yelled, "Mona! Mona!" but got no response.

He staggered from room to room looking for her, but she wasn't there. He went to his liquor cabinet and pulled out a bottle of Hennessey, then plopped down at the bottom of the stairway. He leaned back on the stairs and sat there in silence waiting for Mona to come. He sat there hour after hour, staring at the doorway, but she never showed. He didn't know when he drifted off to sleep. The empty bottle lay beside him.

The next morning, the pain in his back woke him.

Terrance stood. He stretched out his back, hoping the pain would subside. He walked to the front door. He'd left it unlocked, hoping Mona would return, but she hadn't.

Terrance caught a glimpse of himself in a nearby mirror. His shirt was hanging out and his eyes were puffy.

He went upstairs and directly to the bathroom. He turned the water on as hot as he could stand and got under the showerhead. The thought of Mona being with her ex-fiancé was more than he could stand. He beat the shower wall out of frustration. He stayed in the shower until the water ran cold.

Terrance dried off and found some eye drops in the medicine cabinet. He tilted his head back and placed some in each eye. He opened his eyes and looked in the mirror as the redness dissolved.

He dressed in a pair of slacks and a polo shirt. He stopped when he heard a noise outside. He ran to his bedroom window and saw Mona's car pulling away. He didn't see any other vehicles, so he was curious to know if she'd had Garrett drop her off this morning.

He called her cell, but she didn't answer. He finished getting dressed and decided to go into the office because he needed a distraction from his problems.

Terrance felt some comfort when he saw Mona's car parked in front of the office building. He pulled in beside it. He strolled down the walkway, not knowing what he would say when he saw her.

He opened the door, and Mona's back was to him. She was wearing a purple skirt and white blouse, so he knew she'd been home to change. She was fidgeting with the coffeemaker.

"Good morning," Terrance said.

"I just got here, so your coffee should be ready shortly," Mona responded without turning around.

He walked up behind her. "Forget the coffee. We need to discuss last night."

She turned around, and their bodies were so close they were almost touching. He had to reach out to grab her, because she almost stumbled when she turned and noticed he was so close.

She eased away from him, walked to her desk, and took a seat. "I think we both said what we had to say last night."

"Why did you leave with him?" Terrance asked.

"Who I'm with and how I get home is no longer your concern."

"We're a couple, so it will always be my concern."

"I couldn't tell we were a couple the way you allowed your mother to treat me," Mona snapped.

"You lied to me, Mona. What did you expect me to do?" Terrance threw his arms in the air out of frustration.

"You should have waited until we were by ourselves, but instead you aired our business in front of your mom, Garrett, and everyone." Mona's eyes darkened as she talked.

Terrance remembered what had started the whole mess. *Garrett.* "Did you sleep with him?" he blurted.

Mona blinked a few times. "*Excuse* me?"

"Did you sleep with him?"

She laughed. "You sound like your mother."

Terrance slammed his fist on Mona's desk, causing her to jump. "This is not a game. Did you sleep with your ex-fiancé?"

Mona slid her chair away from her desk, increasing the distance between them. "I'm going to give you some time to cool off, and then we will revisit this conversation." She retrieved her purse and keys from her desk drawer.

"Mona, you don't have to leave. The thought of you sleeping with another man is driving me crazy."

"You should have thought about that when you left me to fend for myself." Mona walked out the door.

The coffeemaker buzzed. He turned to see some of the coffee overflowing. "Damn," he said. "This just isn't my day." He rushed to clean the mess.

Chapter Thirty-Six

MONA SAT ACROSS FROM CHARLOTTE'S desk. She'd explained to her what had occurred. She was furious with Terrance, yet upset with herself at the same time for not being honest about Garrett's appearance at the office.

"So do you see my dilemma?" she asked Charlotte.

"You did lie to the man."

"Whose side are you on?" Mona pouted.

"I'm always on your side, and you know that."

"I tried explaining it to him. When his mom started talking, it just got to me. If I didn't get out of there when I did, I would have punched her in the face."

Charlotte laughed. "Yes, in that case, it was definitely best for you to leave when you did."

"I can't help it that Garrett was there to drive me home."

"And you're sure that's all he did?" Charlotte asked.

"Oh, he tried to get me to go back to his hotel, but I wasn't having it."

Charlotte leaned back in her chair. "Things do happen for a reason. I can't believe I'm saying this, but maybe you should explore things with Garrett to make sure that door is closed. The mention of his name still gets you upset, so something must still be there."

Mona tilted her head. "I love Terrance. I loved Garrett at one time, too. A part of me will always love Garrett, but the love I feel for Terrance is much deeper. I hate what happened to Garrett and me, but I can't go backward."

"That's good to hear. So what are you doing here? You should be reassuring Terrance, and then maybe he will stop bombarding my email with all these unrealistic requests." Charlotte laughed and shifted her computer screen.

Mona looked at the screen and saw Terrance's emails. "I'll go make up with him and keep him out your hair, but in the meantime, I suggest you get busy and do your job."

"I'll take care of my business if you can just handle yours."

Mona walked around the desk and gave Charlotte a hug. "I love you too, bestie."

She left Charlotte's office feeling better. She stopped at a little bistro on the way back to the office and picked up food for her and Terrance.

She wasn't expecting to see a huge bouquet of flowers on her desk. She smiled. She carried the bag of food to Terrance's office, and he gave her a cold stare.

"Your boyfriend sent you some flowers. I guess you two must have rekindled things last night," Terrance stated through clenched teeth.

"Last time I checked you were my man, so when did this change?" Mona placed one hand on her hip.

"The moment you slept with your ex."

She slammed the bag of food on his desk. "I came back to make a peace offering, but I see you're still tripping. I didn't sleep with Garrett. But you can think what you want to. And there's your lunch, because I know you haven't eaten anything all day."

Mona stormed out of Terrance's office with tears flowing down her cheeks. She threw the flowers on her desk in the trash, then retrieved her cell phone from her purse and scrolled until she found the number she was looking for.

She leaned on her desk and tapped her foot as the phone rang. She got voicemail. "Garrett, I don't know what kind of game you're playing, but it needs to stop *right now*. I got your flowers but I threw them away, so please stop wasting your money."

Mona dove into work but knew eventually she would have to say something to Terrance, because there were a few messages he needed to respond to.

Once she had calmed down enough to do her job, she knocked on Terrance's door.

"What?" he snapped.

Mona held a folder with printouts in it toward him. He took it.

"These require an immediate response. Inside you will also see your confirmed interview schedule. It's an aggressive schedule. It should keep you busy for the remainder of the week. If you need help with Zoom for the *Roland Martin News One Now* interview, please let me know."

"I'm sure I can handle it."

"Fine. If there's nothing else, I will be working on outlining additional episodes for the sitcom."

"That will be all for now." Terrance refused to look at her.

Mona pouted and walked out.

She sat behind her desk and opened her screenwriting software. She stared at the blank screen for over an hour. Eventually, the ringing phone snapped her out of the trance.

"TNB Productions, how may I help you?" Mona answered.

"I'm surprised you're still there. Terrance should have gotten rid of you."

Mona wasn't going to entertain Sara and her nasty disposition. She placed the call on hold and hit the intercom button. "Your mom's on the line."

She didn't wait for Terrance to respond. She placed the phone on the receiver and turned her attention back to her screen. Her anger seemed to break her writer's block. She began visualizing scenes in her head and started typing the outline for an episode.

Chapter Thirty-Seven

TERRANCE HALF LISTENED TO HIS mother. This was supposed to be a happy time for him, but he was far from happy. He'd lost the woman he loved to her ex-boyfriend, and his mom wouldn't stop nagging him.

Mona's apologies may have been sincere, but why would Garrett be sending her flowers and leaving her a note saying thanks for last night if they hadn't slept together? She'd lied about his visiting the office, so Terrance didn't believe her when she said nothing had happened between them.

He could kick himself, because he'd thought Mona was different from the other women he'd encountered. A part of him now regretted that the network had gone with Mona's idea, because even if he got another assistant, he would be forced to work with her.

He leaned back in his chair and tried to figure out a way to minimize his interactions with Mona. First order of business was to find another assistant. He called Charlotte.

"Terrance, I haven't forgotten about you," Charlotte said.

"Those things can wait. I need your help. I'm looking for a reliable assistant—do you have any suggestions?"

"So you've promoted Mona?" she asked.

"She's going to be working on the series. I'm sure when she gets the check for the signing bonus she'll want to quit."

"I would suggest that you have Mona find her replacement."

That wasn't the response Terrance was looking for. "Okay. I'll do that. Thanks anyway."

He disconnected the call. He didn't want to talk to Mona, so he sent her an email with his request.

Less than five minutes later, she stormed through the door. "Oh, so now you want to fire me and have the nerve to ask *me* to find someone to replace me?"

"Calm down. You're not getting fired," he tried to assure her.

"Then what's with the email?" She crossed her arms, tilted her head, and tapped her right foot.

"You're going to be the head writer. I'll need you to work on the scripts and also help me find other writers to work with you."

She walked closer to the desk. "You should have said that to start with. The email came across as if you were firing me."

"You're transitioning into another role. I've already contacted some other people that I work with on films to see if they will be interested in working behind the scenes with me. That will include payroll, etcetera."

"Looks like you have things covered on your end."

"Our goal is to have our show greenlit for several seasons. This deal is for one season and, based on the ratings, we will renegotiate. So let's put our personal issues aside and get it done. Do you think you can do that?"

"Can *you*?" Mona stared at Terrance without blinking.

He looked away. "Now that we've come to an understanding, will you please start looking for your replacement?"

"I'll get on it right away."

Terrance pretended to look at his computer screen. Mona's spunky attitude was a turn-on. It almost made him forget her betrayal.

He looked up, and she was gone.

This time Terrance actually read what was on his computer screen. He opened the email from Mona. She'd written, *Thanks for breaking my heart. Hope you enjoy being single again!!!*

She came back into his office. "When you come to work tomorrow, please bring the bag I left at your place."

"Why don't you come by and get it tonight?" Terrance asked.

She shook her head. "Under the circumstances, I don't think it would be a good idea." She looked at the clock and then back at him. "You better go. You have an interview on The Foxxhole. If you leave now, you'll be there on time."

She walked out without saying another word. Terrance felt like a heel. Even though he'd been harsh with her earlier, she'd still managed to take care of him. He had forgotten about the interview. She'd given him the schedule, but he'd barely looked at it. His phone beeped to alert him of the appointment. Mona had thought of everything. She'd synced his appointments to alert him on his phone.

He gathered everything he would need to read over at home later and left the office.

Mona seemed to be in a deep conversation on the phone, so he waved at her. She didn't wave back. He continued out the door.

Two hours later, he was laughing as he wrapped up his interview with the show's host. Terrance enjoyed sharing his news with the audience. It felt good to have the respect of someone whose career he'd admired for years.

Terrance soon felt the weight of his decision to end things with Mona. Maybe he had overreacted to the situation. He was second-guessing the decision as he drove home.

Chapter Thirty-Eight

MONA HIT THE PUNCHING BAG at the back of the gym with an intensity that surprised Jeff, one of the trainers.

"Who are you mad at?" he asked.

"Nobody." Mona punched the bag harder.

"That's right. Get it off your chest," Kem said, from behind her.

Mona turned to the side and saw Kem wiping sweat from her forehead. "How did you enjoy the Zumba class?"

"I'm thinking about becoming a regular."

"I wasn't in the mood to dance." Mona hit the bag again.

"Obviously not. Do you want to talk about it?" Kem asked.

"Sure. We're done here, I think. Aren't we, Jeff?"

"Yes. I'll see you next time." Jeff grabbed his towel and bottled water and left them alone.

"Let me grab my stuff and then we can walk over to the coffee shop and talk," Mona said.

Kem remained quiet while listening to Mona talk about what had occurred in the previous twenty-four hours.

"I'm sorry. I think you and Terrance make a good couple."

"We *did* make a good couple. He ended things with me, remember?"

"Once he has time to think, he'll be calling you, and you can work things out."

Mona sipped on her cappuccino. "I don't know. You didn't see or hear him. The flowers were pretty. I hated I had to throw them in the trash, but under the circumstances, I thought it was best."

"You can't keep ignoring Garrett. I think you need to meet with him one more time and make it clear that you don't want him."

"Maybe you're right. Maybe I've gone about this the wrong way. I'll invite him over for dinner, and then he and I can talk."

Kem frowned. "You know what? I'm jealous. I've never been invited over to your place. I've dropped you off, but never have you invited me inside."

"That's because my little place doesn't compare to yours."

"Whatever. I couldn't care less about the size of something. We're friends."

"I know, but I love hanging out at yours and Charlotte's place because it gives me a chance to see another side of life. Don't get me wrong, I'm not starving. I'm living within my means, but I do want a bigger place."

"With this new series, something tells me that you'll be moving to a new address real soon. People are already talking."

Mona smiled. "So there's buzz?"

"I'm so happy for you."

"It could have happened sooner if you-know-who had given me a spot on their writing team."

Kem pretended to not know what Mona was referring to. "You know I keep my business and personal life separate."

"I know. I wish I would have. Now I'm forced to work with a man who doesn't want me anymore." Mona started sniffling.

Kem placed her hand over Mona's. "It's going to be all right. Don't cry. If you cry, I'm going to cry."

Mona moved her hand and wiped her eyes. "I'm not going to cry. I'm going to pull myself together and make this work."

"That's the stuff." Kem's phone beeped. "I've got a late-night staff meeting, so I'll catch you later."

"Sure thing," Mona responded.

She watched Kem leave, then pulled out her cell phone and sent a text message to Garrett inviting him over.

Mona heard a knock on the door. She sprayed floral air freshener in the air. She put on some lip-gloss, held her head down, and shook her head so her curls could fall. She wasn't interested in Garrett, but she still wanted to look cute. She glanced at herself in the mirror and pulled down her black knit top so that it went past the belt loops of her black jeans. Satisfied with how she looked, she went and opened the door.

Garrett stood on the other side wearing slacks and a turtleneck sweater. His fashion sense was totally opposite from Terrance's, Mona noted.

"Come in."

He gripped a bottle of wine. "I didn't know what you were serving, but white wine goes with everything."

"Thanks." Mona took the bottle from him.

He looked around. "Cute place."

"Small, I know. But I'm on a budget and don't like living beyond my means."

"It's still cute," Garrett responded.

"I guess. Dinner's ready. As you can see, I only have enough room for a small table, so it'll be a little cozy."

"Cozy is good." He smiled.

Mona had cooked a quick meal, spaghetti and meatballs. She served it with some salad and garlic bread.

Garrett took a bite out of his food. "It's better than the last meal you tried to cook for me, that's for sure."

Mona laughed. "Back then I couldn't boil water."

"But you were going to be marrying a doctor. I would have hired you a cook. It was either that or starve." Garrett laughed.

The playful banter continued over dinner. Eventually, Mona put the dirty dishes in the dishwasher and then sat next to Garrett on the couch.

"I really appreciate you giving us a chance to talk. I've missed you over the years. I really have." He took her hand and kissed the back of it. She pulled away.

"Life without you was hard at first, but I learned to adjust."

"I'm here now. We can fulfill our destiny. The way things were supposed to be. Do you feel me?" Garrett's eyes were filled with love.

Mona felt her heart soften toward him. She placed her hand on the side of his face. "Garrett, at one time you were the man I'd planned to spend my life with, and I wish things had worked out. Your mom changed the wheel of destiny when she interfered."

She wasn't prepared for his tears. The sound of his pain tugged at her guts. Before she realized it, her arms were around him, comforting him. He pulled away slightly and then kissed her.

Mona closed her eyes and imagined Garrett was Terrance. The intensity of the kiss increased. She opened her eyes, and her temporary fantasy was interrupted by reality. Garrett was not Terrance, and they had no business kissing. She pushed him away and jumped off the couch.

"I hope he's worth it," he said. "His mom seems like a piece of work."

"This isn't about Terrance. We're two different people now. Maybe if we'd married we could have grown together, but it didn't work out that way. I'm sorry."

"I'm sorry too. I promise to respect your wishes going forward. Can we at least be friends?" Garrett asked.

"Maybe in due time. For now, let's play it by ear."

"I hope Terrance gets his act together, because he's one lucky man." He stood and walked toward the door, then turned around and looked at her. "Goodbye, Mona. All I want is for you to be happy."

"Overall, I am. I want you to be happy too. Allow yourself to love someone else. You have my permission, okay?" Mona smiled and placed her hand over his heart.

She gave Garrett a goodbye hug. They both knew this was the end of their chapter.

Chapter Thirty-Nine

TERRANCE SAT IN HIS CAR and went back and forth in his mind on whether he should go to Mona's place. Finally, he'd decided to bring her bag over. It would give him an excuse to talk to her outside of the office.

He was prepared to get out of his car when he saw her door open. He then saw her hug Garrett. He hit his steering wheel. So now his fears had been confirmed. Mona had lied about not sleeping with Garrett. This was the confirmation he needed.

He started the engine of his SUV and sped away, flying down the highway twenty miles over the speed limit. He didn't care until he saw the flashing red lights in his rearview mirror.

He hit the steering wheel again and pulled his SUV to the side of the road. He rolled down his window. The officer shined his flashlight in Terrance's face.

"I clocked you going eighty miles per hour in a fifty-five-mile-an-hour zone. Let me see your license and registration."

"My wallet is right here on the dashboard. I'm going to reach for it and hand it to you. My license and proof of insurance are right there."

"Okay, sir. Remove them and hand them both to me. I also need to see your registration. This is an expensive SUV, so I need to confirm you're the owner."

"I'll need to go in the glove compartment for it."

"Go ahead." The officer held his hand on his gun with one hand and shined the flashlight with the other as he watched Terrance move a sheet of paper.

The officer eased back when Terrance handed him his vehicle registration.

"You stay here. I'll be right back."

Terrance watched the officer in his rearview mirror. The officer got in his police cruiser and a few minutes later returned.

"You're clear. I'll have to write you a ticket for speeding. If you want to contest it, the instructions are on the back."

"I understand."

Terrance took the speeding ticket and pulled away. He was glad the traffic stop had ended with no incident.

He made a conscious effort to watch his speed. His plans to drive around had changed when he was stopped by the police officer; instead of cruising, he went directly home.

He pulled out a bottle of bourbon from under the cabinet, grabbed a glass, and went to the living room. He flipped stations and landed on the movie *Titanic*. He poured himself glass after glass and watched the movie, a tragic love story—a phrase that also currently described his life. He emptied the bottle out and fell back on the couch.

The next morning, his phone buzzed constantly until it finally woke him out of his sleep.

Terrance reached for the phone. When he saw the alert, he jumped, hitting his toe on the coffee table. "Ouch," he yelled.

He had less than fifteen minutes to get dressed and make it to the local TV affiliate for his national interview. He didn't have time to shower, so he wiped his face, brushed his teeth, and gargled several times. He placed both hands over his mouth and blew to make sure his breath didn't smell like alcohol. As an extra precaution, he gargled with the mouthwash again.

Fortunately, his clothes were well organized in his huge walk-in closet. He put on a gray Armani suit with a pair of matching oxford shoes. He tilted his head to make sure he didn't need to shave. He looked like a million bucks.

He only had a few minutes to prepare after arriving at the studio. One of the makeup artists fanned his face with a brush. She said, "You were shining. Now you're perfect."

On the studio floor, Patricia Bell, one of the local reporters, said, "The affiliate will be bouncing to us in a few seconds. Are you ready?"

Terrance nodded. "Ready."

Patricia read from the autocue and then began asking Terrance questions about his new show and other projects. The interview only lasted ten minutes, but it felt like hours to Terrance, because he knew his interview would be seen by the millions of people who watched the *Early Morning Show*.

At the end of the interview, Patricia thanked him, and then Terrance went straight to the office to set up his Zoom call. The interview with Roland Martin went well and without any technical glitches on his end. He checked his phone to see if he had any more appointments. His next interview was with a magazine reporter. It was scheduled during lunchtime.

The front office door opened. It was only seven in the morning, so he jumped out of his chair to see who'd entered.

"Oh it's you," Terrance said when he saw Mona drape her jacket over her chair.

"Good morning to you too," she responded.

"I wasn't expecting you so early," he confessed.

"I couldn't sleep, so I thought I would come in and get an early start."

Mona went about her normal morning routine of making coffee. Terrance wanted to reach out to her and hold her, but then he remembered what he'd seen the night before. The anger and hurt he felt returned, and he left Mona alone as he returned to his office.

Terrance closed his door. How was he going to be able to work so close to the woman who was tearing his heart apart? He wanted Mona and didn't want to lose her to her ex. He had to think of *something*, because this wedge between them was driving him crazy.

His cell rang. He went to his desk and saw his mother's number on the screen. He wasn't in the mood to deal with her, so he sent her call to voicemail. Then the office phone rang. Mona's voice came over the intercom. He hit the button and responded, "I'm not here."

He sat in his chair and swiveled it around with his back toward the desk. He closed his eyes and mediated. He felt better and was able to concentrate on work. He made a few phone calls to some of his crew members.

By the time he'd finished with the phone calls, it was time for him to leave for another interview. He walked out of the door and couldn't help but notice Mona's face. She seemed just as sad as he felt.

Chapter Forty

IT'D BEEN SEVERAL WEEKS SINCE Mona said her final goodbye to Garrett. He'd honored their agreement and hadn't contacted her. Being around Terrance frustrated her. One minute he was nice to her, and the next he was snapping off her head. She never knew which version of Terrance she would get.

She hadn't chosen a replacement yet. She was thinking about using the help of a staffing agency to find her replacement if the next few interviews didn't go well. She needed someone quick, because Terrance had seemed to double her workload.

Mona felt miserable. This was supposed to be one of the best times of her life.

The door opened and she smiled. Entering was a woman who was about Mona's height. Mona admired how nice she was dressed in her navy-blue skirt suit.

"Welcome to TNB Productions." Mona stood and extended her hand to the woman.

"Hi. I'm Catherine and I'm here for the secretary position." The woman had a really soft voice. Mona strained to hear her.

"Have a seat." Mona touched a chair in front of her desk.

The woman did as instructed.

Mona glanced at Catherine's résumé. "How long did you work as Pat Barnes's assistant?"

Quietly, the woman responded, "One week."

Mona could barely hear her. She moved her chair closer and tilted her head to the side. "Can you repeat that?"

"One week," Catherine repeated.

"Do you have a cold or something?"

"No. I'm perfectly healthy."

Mona wished she had a megaphone to hand to her. "Let's try something else. I'm going to call the phone, and I want you to show me how you would answer it."

Mona pulled out her cell phone and dialed the office. Catherine smiled, leaned forward, and said *something* into the phone. Mona looked at her phone and then at Catherine. "I want you to tell me about your drive over here today."

She could see Catherine's lips moving. She could even hear a slight sound coming out of her mouth, but couldn't hear her.

"That's enough. Catherine, thank you for coming, but I don't think you're a fit for TNB Productions. I do wish you well on your next endeavor."

"Thank you. Maybe if another position opens, you will consider me," Catherine said.

Mona smiled and shook her head. After that interview, she thought she needed to test her hearing.

She called Kem. It sounded like Kem was yelling when she answered. Mona decreased the volume on her phone. "Thank God I can hear," she said.

"What are you talking about?" Kem asked.

"I'll tell you later. I have another appointment." Mona ended the call with Kem and waited for the next candidate.

Based on their résumés, the next few interviews seemed promising. The next candidate walked through the door. Her perfume filled the room the moment she entered. It would have been okay, but it had a pungent, musky smell to it. Mona twitched her nose and held out her hand.

"Welcome to TNB Productions."

"Thank you, I'm Janie. Nice to meet you."

"Have a seat." Mona kept putting her hand to her nose. "I see on your résumé that you worked at Wally World for ten years. Why are you now looking for new employment?"

"I've been working the night shift, and I'm also tired of doing the same old thing. With a job like this, it'll give me some variety."

"Okay, I understand."

"May I ask you something?" Janie said. "You may not notice, but there's a strange smell in here. You may want to spray or something."

Mona had an "are you serious?" look on her face. "I will be sure to spray as soon as you leave." She meant it. But she couldn't take any more of the stench. "Janie, I have a few more candidates to check out before making my decision. If you don't hear from me by tomorrow, then regrettably, that means we went with someone else."

Mona almost passed out because she was trying to hold her breath while she talked.

Janie stood, and the smell almost knocked Mona out of her chair. "I understand. You have all my numbers."

Mona reached in her desk, pulled out the air freshener, and sprayed the moment Janie stepped out of the office. She sprayed all around the room. She coughed a few times because the fumes got in her nostrils.

She got a chair and stood on it, then sprayed the air freshener in the vent and got down. The door opened—her next appointment had arrived. Mona stared at the woman in a tight, fitted dress that accented all of her curves.

"I'm Cindy," the curvaceous woman said.

"I know exactly who you are," Mona said. "If I would have known it was you, I could have saved you the trip."

"Excuse me? Maybe you got me confused with someone else. I'm here to interview for the assistant job."

"Cindy Scott. University of California. Majored in English lit." Mona recognized Cindy as one of the mean girls. Mona's parents weren't rich, so she hadn't had the luxury of having her own car and expensive designer clothes like Cindy and her crew. Mona had walked in on Cindy and some of her friends talking about her on many occasions.

"I'm sorry, but I really don't recognize who you are—but obviously, you know of me."

"Remember the poor Black Texas girl you and your friends teased? Well, I am she, and I'm no longer shy and timid. Thanks to you girls, I grew up, and fast."

Cindy giggled. "We were young then. I didn't know any better. Since then, I've changed. I've changed a lot."

"I'm sure you have, but as far as you're concerned, the job you applied for has already been fulfilled."

"B-but…" Cindy stammered.

Mona went to the door and opened it. "Either you leave voluntarily or I will throw you out."

"I know what it is. You're still the same insecure little girl from Texas. Most women are intimidated by me, so I understand." Cindy swooped her long weave over her shoulder and sashayed out the door.

"Good riddance," Mona said, and shut the door.

She sat behind the computer feeling defeated as the door opened and the last candidate scheduled for the day entered. Mona checked out the young lady from head to toe. She nodded her approval of the woman's attire.

"Hi. I'm Jerricka Thomas. I'm here to see Mona."

Mona got out of her seat. Jerricka was on time, dressed well, and had a nice voice that she didn't have to strain to hear. She shook her hand. "Have a seat."

Mona went through the interview questions, and Jerricka answered each one in a satisfactory manner. After the interview she said, "There's one other person you need to meet. Can you give me a minute and let me see if he's available?"

"Sure." Jerricka crossed her legs.

Mona knocked on Terrance's door and entered. "I have a young lady I would like for you to interview for the assistant position. Do you have a moment?" she asked.

Terrance barely looked up when he responded, "Send her in."

Mona hated the tension between them. She plastered on a fake smile, turned around, and said to Jerricka, "Terrance will see you now. I'll be waiting right here when you get out."

She exhaled. It had been a busy morning. She crossed her fingers. Hopefully Terrance liked Jerricka too and it would help ease the tension between them.

Chapter Forty-One

TERRANCE NEEDED TO STOP BEING stubborn and forgive Mona. He missed their friendship. He missed her snarky comments. He missed her input on his projects. Seeing her in the office every day and not being able to talk to her the way he used to was torture.

He lifted his head when the young lady Mona had mentioned walked in. He stood and greeted her. "I'm Terrance Beckham, and you must be Jerricka."

"Yes, sir," she responded.

"Have a seat and tell me a little about yourself."

"I recently graduated from USC. I majored in business but took some film classes, and I thought it would be great to work with an established producer and learn as much as I can."

Terrance listened to Jerricka tell him about her background. She reminded him of himself when he was her age.

"As my assistant, you will have a lot of responsibility. You'll be my office manager and must be available for functions that usually take place outside of the nine-to-five work window."

"I understand. If you hire me, you will get a worker bee, and I'll make myself available to you twenty-four seven."

Terrance laughed. "I'm sure I won't need you *every* hour of the day, but it's good to know. I will get with Mona and she will give you a call once we make our final decision."

"Thanks."

Terrance walked Jerricka to the door and watched her say her goodbyes to Mona.

Mona turned and faced him. "So what did you think?" she asked.

"How do *you* feel?"

"She's perfect. I wanted someone with a little more office experience, but I think her eagerness to learn is a plus. Out of everyone I interviewed, she's the best candidate."

"After you verify her references and do a background check, if she pans out, I say we hire her."

"Let me get on that right away," Mona said.

Terrance stood there and stared at her.

"Is there anything else?"

"Yes, there is."

Terrance pushed all of his negative feelings to the side, took Mona in his arms, and kissed her passionately. She kissed him back with the same intensity.

She pulled back for a moment. "Wait."

"Mona, don't. I need you. I need this."

She walked to the door and locked it, then faced him and seductively grabbed him by the collar. "Now, where were we?"

Terrance covered her lips with his. His hands roamed all over her body. They moved until they were near Mona's desk. Without stopping, he used one hand and cleared an area on Mona's desk. He lifted her and placed her on the desk. He eased her skirt over her hips. He removed her panties with one hand. He used his fingers to make love to her. The moisture he felt turned him on. He replaced his fingers with his mouth.

Terrance eased his tongue in and out and twirled it around slow and then fast. He continued those motions until he felt Mona's legs tremble.

She screamed out in pleasure. "Terrance. Oh, Terrance," she said over and over as she climaxed in his mouth.

Terrance unbuckled his pants and, without taking them completely off, eased his boxers down and positioned himself. He got harder the moment he felt the moisture between Mona's legs.

He opened her blouse and freed one of her breasts. He wrapped his lips around her nipple. The more he sucked, the wetter she got and the harder he became. He enjoyed hearing her moans. They turned him on even more. He stopped suckling on her breast and placed his head on her chest as he pumped in and out of her. He closed his eyes and got lost in her sweetness.

They both moaned and groaned with pleasure. Terrance felt himself losing control. Mona wrapped her legs around his waist and they climaxed together.

"I still love you," Terrance said as he pulled away. He fastened his pants and left Mona to go to his office.

She stormed in the room still looking a little disheveled. "What was *that* all about?" she asked.

"I don't know," Terrance confessed.

"When you figure it out, let me know." Without another word, Mona left his office and slammed the door shut.

The painting on the wall shook.

Terrance leaned back in his chair. He inhaled. He could still smell Mona's fragrance on his lips. He needed to swallow his pride and make things right with her, but he was a man who didn't want to share. He wanted Mona all to himself, and he wasn't sure she was ready to let her past go.

Chapter Forty-Two

LATER ON THAT DAY, MONA sat at the coffee shop talking with Charlotte. "I wish Kem could have been here," she said.

"She's filming the fall season finale for her show," Charlotte responded.

"Oh, I forgot. Next year, that will be me." Mona beamed on the inside.

"I'm happy for you and Terrance." Charlotte sipped on her espresso.

"Ugh." Mona sighed. She revealed to Charlotte everything that had transpired between her and Terrance. She'd previously kept some things from her friend, because with Charlotte being Terrance's manager, Mona didn't want to get her in the middle of things.

"All of what's going on with you two is nothing but a big misunderstanding. Just like Sean and me, you two are destined to be together," Charlotte proclaimed.

"I thought that too. But now I'm not so sure."

Charlotte leaned forward. "Someone needs to be the bigger person and make the first move. Don't allow pride to stand in the way of your being happy."

Mona recounted to Charlotte her and Terrance's last conversation. "I asked him what it meant, and he said he didn't know. So what am I supposed to do now?"

"I'm going to tell you what you told me about Sean: go get your man. Terrance wants you, or else he wouldn't have reached out to you in that manner."

"Of course he wants me—what man wouldn't?" Mona smiled, getting back some of her spunk.

"See, now that's the Mona I know. Go get him, girl." Charlotte lifted her glass in the air.

Mona tapped Charlotte's glass with hers. But she wished she felt as confident as she pretended to be.

She went home, showered, and dressed. She stopped got Chinese food from one of Terrance's favorite restaurants, then parked behind his car in his driveway. She took a glance at herself in the rearview mirror.

"You can do this," she said.

Before she could change her mind, she got out of the car with the bags of food. She slowly made her way toward the door.

Should I or shouldn't I? Mona asked herself as she stood at the door contemplating whether to ring the doorbell.

The more she thought about it, the more she thought that her being there wasn't a good idea.

But before she could leave, the door swung open. Terrance stood there with a frown on his face. "I've been standing here for five minutes waiting for you to ring the doorbell," he said.

"I… W-well," she stammered. She held out the bag. "I come in peace."

"Come on in." Terrance took the bag from her and moved out of the way so she could enter.

"People say a way to a man's heart is through his stomach, so I'm hoping that's true." Mona looked into Terrance's eyes, hoping to see a glimmer of hope.

His eyes twinkled. "You didn't have to bring food from my favorite spot, but since you did, let's eat."

She followed him to the kitchen and took a seat at the table, and watched him remove the items from the bag. The tension between them remained thick. Mona would sneak a glance at Terrance and she would catch him glancing at her, but neither said a word while eating.

She stared at the last bite of food, played with it with her plastic fork.

"Mona, look at me," Terrance commanded.

She looked into eyes that had now softened.

He reached across the table and took her hand.

"I pushed my pride to the side to come here, so be gentle," Mona blurted.

Terrance tilted his head to the side. "Baby, I'm glad you're here. Do you know how hard it's been to see you at the office and not be able to hug you, kiss you, or hold you like I want to?"

Mona sat speechless.

Terrance continued. "I've been asking myself ever since I left the office what I wanted, and life without you has been miserable. I can't tell you how many times I've held the phone to call you, but didn't."

Mona could relate. She'd been doing the same thing. "Why didn't you call?"

"Every time I got ready to, I remembered seeing Garrett kiss you."

She frowned. "Terrance, what are you talking about?"

"The day you asked for your clothes. That night, I dropped by to bring them to you. You'd never invited me inside before, so imagine my surprise when I saw Garrett walking out. But not only did I see him walking out, I saw him kissing you."

"Garrett wasn't kissing me. We were hugging." She only told the partial truth, because Garrett *had* kissed her when they were seated on the couch earlier.

"But I swore that's what I saw. Do you know how torn I was? I was so pissed I sped away and got stopped by a cop."

Mona's hand flew to her mouth. "Oh no."

"I'm not tripping about that. Even though I told you I didn't want us anymore, I lied. I want you. I want us. I know I've been acting like a jackass with you lately, and I promise to change that. I've already given my competition leeway, but now I'm about to close the gap."

Terrance stood, leaned forward, and kissed Mona on the lips.

"Terrance, what are you saying?"

"I want you back, and if it means *proving* that I'm better than Garrett, I'm willing to do it."

Mona opened her mouth to confess that Garrett wasn't in the picture, but decided not to. Maybe Terrance should continue to think he was. It was his penance for all of the agony he'd put her through.

Chapter Forty-Three

TERRANCE HADN'T PLANNED ON GROVELING and begging Mona to be with him. If his friends knew about this, he would lose his man card. But at this point, he didn't care about being macho—he just wanted his woman back, and if it took swallowing his pride to do so, then so be it.

He'd planned on showing Mona that Garrett couldn't give her the type of life she deserved. Besides, Mona was his. She'd been his from the first time they'd made love, whether she knew it or not.

She started helping him clean off the table, but he stopped her. "I got this. Why don't you go chill in the living room, and I'll be there in a minute."

Mona didn't protest. She left him alone. As soon as she left the room, Terrance went into romance mode. He removed a cold bottle of champagne from the refrigerator and located two flutes.

He placed them on the counter, then went outside and picked a few roses from his rosebush. He grabbed the champagne and then rushed up the back stairway from the kitchen and into his bedroom. He tore rose petals and spread them across the bed.

He rushed to the top of the stairs and yelled Mona's name out several times until she appeared below.

"Can you meet me upstairs for a minute?"

"Sure," she responded.

Terrance went to the bedroom and stood in the doorway. He watched Mona with anticipation as she took each step. The closer she got to him, the faster his heart beat.

"I wanted to talk to you about something," he said.

He moved out of the way, and Mona gasped in surprise when she saw the rose petals on the floor and bed.

"Were you expecting someone else and I just happened to show?" she asked.

"No, baby. I just did this," Terrance assured her. "This is all for you."

He went to the nightstand, popped the cork off the champagne, and poured it into the flutes. He handed one to Mona and held on to one. "To a new beginning."

Mona tapped his flute. They both took sips. She said, "The roses were a nice touch. You know how much I like flowers."

"I know." Terrance grabbed her hand and led her to the bed. He took the glass from her and placed it on the bedside table.

"There's something I want to tell you," Mona said.

"Shh. Right now, there's nothing you can say that will change my mind about us."

"Maybe you should hear this."

Terrance didn't want to hear Garrett's name. He covered her mouth with his and took her breath away. They both fell back on the bed. As they continued the kiss, he used one of his hands to unfasten her pants. His attempt to remove them was unsuccessful. He laughed to himself.

"These things are skintight. I may need some help," Terrance joked.

"Only if you do a strip show for me." Mona stared at him with a smile on her face.

"Oh, you want a show? I'll give it to you. But by the end of my performance, I want to see *you* naked."

Terrance seductively removed his clothing, dancing. Mona yelled, "That's it. If I had some dollars, I would be making it rain right about now."

They both laughed. Terrance had missed this playful banter they had with one another. Even before they'd gotten involved romantically, they were able to have fun around the office. He'd missed this side of Mona and was enjoying seeing her smile and laugh again.

Mona removed her tight jeans and shirt and lay on top of the rose petals on the bed, naked, by the time he'd removed his boxers. He wasn't sure if she was prepared for him, but she should be able to see by looking at his erection that he was *more* than ready for her.

Terrance kissed Mona, eased his fingers inside of her. He got harder when he felt how moist she was. She was ready for him. He positioned himself on top of her. Her eyes were closed.

"Look at me, Mona. I want to see your eyes when I enter you."

Without waiting for her to respond, he went inside her. She gasped in pleasure. He got lost in her eyes as he made love to her as if his life depended on it. She placed her legs on top of his shoulders, and he went deeper and deeper inside of her. Moans of pleasure filled the room.

Terrance closed his eyes and felt himself losing control as he deep-stroked her. Mona wrapped her legs around his waist and dug her fingernails into his back. He felt her legs shake and released his seed inside of her.

"I've missed you," he whispered.

"I've missed you too."

Chapter Forty-Four

MONA PINCHED HERSELF TO MAKE sure she wasn't dreaming. Terrance lay next to her snoring. She leaned on her side and watched him. They'd made love several times throughout the night. Terrance had definitely put in some overtime, and her body was a little sore, but it was worth it.

She'd tried to come clean with him about Garrett. She wanted him to know that Garrett wasn't competition because he was no longer a part of her life.

She slipped from underneath the covers, then went to the bathroom and ran herself a bubble bath. The hot water soothed her muscles the moment she sat in the tub. She leaned back and closed her eyes, but opened them when she heard the door open.

Terrance walked in wearing nothing but his boxers. "You should have woken me. We could have bathed together," he said.

"It's still not too late." Mona held bubbles in her hand and blew them in his direction.

Terrance removed his shorts and got in the huge, sauna-sized bathtub. They took turns washing each other. The intimacy drew them closer together. Mona faced Terrance. He cupped one of her breasts with his hand after washing it. He wrapped his lips around her nipple and flicked his tongue back and forth.

She eased on top of Terrance's erection. The water sloshed with their movements. Mona's head fell back. Right now she was in total bliss.

"I love you," they moaned in unison.

Terrance held her by the waist as they climaxed together.

Later, in Terrance's room, Mona said, "I'll have to meet you in the office later. I need to go by my place and change clothes."

"Wait right here." Terrance went to his closet and returned holding a hanger with one of her pantsuits, and in his other hand he held some of her underwear. "These were in the hamper and I just never returned them."

Mona took them from him. "So what were you going to do with my panties? Keep them as a souvenir?"

"I would have returned them. Eventually," Terrance responded with a smirk.

"Yeah, right." She slipped on her underwear.

"Let me help you with that." He walked behind Mona to assist her with her bra. He cupped her breasts with his hands and pinched her nipples.

"Don't start something you can't finish," she teased.

Terrance moved her hair and kissed the back of her neck. "You know I can finish anything I start."

"Don't you have an interview with the reporter from *Ebony* around ten?"

"Saved by an interview." He stopped kissing her, grabbed each side of her bra, and snapped it into place.

Mona dressed while Terrance went to his closet and dressed. When he came out, she gave him a once-over. "Looking good, mister."

"Just in case they want to snap some photos. Maybe you should come with me. Plus, if it wasn't for your script, I might not be getting this opportunity."

"You're good, so the network would have worked with you regardless."

"Come on, Mona. I need you there for moral support," Terrance said.

"I have things to do, like approve the final payment on the last movie you worked on."

"Oh yeah, I forgot about that. See, that's why you're good for me. I hope the new assistant is just as competent as you are."

"I'm sure she will be. I checked her references. I'll make her an official offer today."

"Good. Well, it's close to time. I'll walk you out." Terrance held the bedroom door open.

Mona practically skipped into the office. Since Terrance had the interview, she would be by herself for the next few hours. The flower delivery guy stopped by for the second time today. He'd just delivered a nice tropical bouquet of flowers an hour before.

"I'm back," he said.

"I see. What do you have this time?" Mona asked.

He handed her a box of Godiva chocolate candy and a single red rose.

Mona reached into her purse to give him a tip.

The delivery guy refused to take it. "The tip's already been taken care of."

Mona read the card on the box. *The single red rose is because you're the only one with my heart. This box of chocolate is because you're so sweet.* It was signed *T.*

"Aw," she sighed.

Mona hadn't eaten anything, and after her morning lovemaking session with Terrance, she was starving. She removed the plastic from the box of candy and took one out. She chewed on it like it was the best piece of chocolate she'd ever tasted. She ate two more pieces before closing the box and placing it on the opposite side of her desk.

She finished approving the payroll and made the deadline with ten minutes to spare. A text from Terrance indicated he would be gone all day due to a photoshoot with the magazine.

His presence wasn't forgotten, though, because over the next few hours, Mona received more flowers, a teddy bear, and an assortment of fruit from Terrance. His outward displays of affection had worked on erasing some of the doubts she had about his being ready for a commitment.

Chapter Forty-Five

TERRANCE'S DAY HADN'T GONE AS planned, but he found himself enjoying the photoshoot. He'd only expected to be gone for two hours for the interview. But the *Ebony* reporter had ideas of doing a photoshoot in Santa Barbara.

He wished he could have been there to see Mona's expression after she received the deliveries. He smiled when he got her text messages expressing her gratitude.

Eventually, Terrance hit the highway. He called Mona. "Dress in something sexy. I'm taking you out tonight."

"What time do you want me to meet you?"

"Seven will be fine, and I'm picking you up at your place. Well, unless there's a reason why you don't want me to?" he asked.

"Of course I don't mind. Call me when you get downstairs and I'll come out," she said.

They ended the call. Terrance felt a twinge of jealousy. *Garrett* got to go inside. Why didn't he have the same privilege?

He needed to snap himself out of it. He'd never been an insecure man, and he wasn't about to start now. He knew he was what Mona needed, and would continue to woo her so she would know it for herself.

Terrance took Mona to his favorite Japanese restaurant. The dim lights gave it a romantic ambience. They were led to their own private room. The waiter held out Mona's chair for her.

"I've heard about this place, but it's my first time coming here," she said.

"The food is good. You'll love it." Terrance took a seat across from her.

The waiter took their drink orders and handed them each a menu.

Mona glanced at the selections. "Since you've been here before, I'll let you order for me."

"Oh, you trust me to do that?"

"It's a test to see if you know me as well as you think you do." Mona winked. She placed the menu in front of her.

Terrance placed their orders when the waiter returned.

Mona's smile outshone the flickering candles. "You surprised me today with all of the deliveries. Very creative, too, with the notes."

"I can be romantic when I try to be." He winked.

"And to think you did it all by yourself, without me having to do it for you. That's what made it more special."

"I am helpless without you."

"Terrance, your flattery will get you everywhere."

They both laughed.

Mona's cell rang. She glanced at it and placed it back in her purse.

"You could have answered," Terrance said.

"It was my sister, and I'm not talking to her right now."

"Do tell."

"She and I always get into it, so it's nothing. Tomorrow, we'll be saying we love one another."

"Are you sure?" Terrance asked.

"Positive. If it was about my parents, she would have texted me nine-one-one, and she hasn't, so whatever else she has to say can wait."

"I just had an idea. Before things start getting hectic around here with our schedules, why don't you take a trip home? And, of course, I'll tag along."

"It's not in my budget," Mona admitted.

"With the money you'll be making from the sitcom, money will no longer be an issue for you. Besides, I suggested the trip because it's my treat."

She looked puzzled. "I don't know. You and I are still trying to figure us out. If I take a guy home to my parents, they will think it's more serious than it is."

"At least think about it." Terrance hid his disappointment.

"I'll think about it and let you know." Mona took the last bite of her food.

"Would you like to go dancing?" he asked.

"After eating all of this, I do need some exercise." Mona looked at the empty dishes in front of them on the table.

"I have the perfect spot in mind."

After leaving the restaurant, he drove them to a popular club. The line to gain access was wrapped around the corner. Terrance, with Mona beside him, bypassed the long line and went directly to the front. He whispered something into the bouncer's ear and slipped him a couple of twenty-dollar bills.

"Right this way," the bouncer said, moving out of the way so they could enter.

Terrance heard curse words from some of the people who had been waiting in line.

"Ooh, that's my song," Mona said, grabbing his hand and leading him to the dance floor the moment they stepped through the doors.

They danced to three songs before the deejay came on the PA. "We're going to slow it down a little. This is a new joint by Sean

Maxwell. So fellas, grab your ladies and let them know you love them."

Terrance wrapped his arms around Mona's waist and pulled her close to him, and they swayed along to the slow jam. He stared into her eyes. Her luscious red lips were inviting. He forgot they were out in public and kissed her. She laid her head on his chest. He wondered if she could hear his heartbeat, just like the song said.

Without Mona, he felt incomplete. Now that he'd given in to his feelings for her, he didn't want to lose her. He would do everything it took to hold on to her.

The song ended. "I'm thirsty," Mona said.

Terrance looked around. "There's a table right there." He pointed. "I'll grab us some drinks and meet you there."

He stuck out his chest with pride as he watched other men admire Mona. He smiled because he knew she was with him, so the other men could look, but they were not able to touch.

Chapter Forty-Six

MONA HAD NEVER FELT LOVED the way she did now. In just twenty-four hours, her life with Terrance was back on track. His outpouring of love had amazed her. She was glad she'd listened to Charlotte.

But she'd almost stuttered when Terrance asked about her sister. He didn't need to know that her sister had given Garrett her contact information without checking with her or warning her that he'd reached out. She would deal with her sister when she was in the mood to.

Mona thought about Terrance's offer. The idea of visiting Texas was enticing.

"Mona, what are you doing here?" Garrett asked, standing in front of her in the club.

"Garrett?" Mona was surprised to see him.

He took a seat next to her without bothering to ask for her permission.

"Good to see you. I wondered if I would ever see you again."

"Garrett, I thought you'd given up hopes of you and I being together."

"I agreed to let you go, but there's always hope."

"No, there isn't." Mona shook her head.

"Can I at least have this dance?" Garrett asked, ignoring all of the signs that she didn't want him sitting at the table with her.

"No, you may not," Terrance said from behind. "She's here with me."

Garrett stood. "She doesn't belong to you."

"Mona's not a piece of property meant to be owned."

Mona liked seeing Terrance stand up for her.

Garrett looked at her. "Are you here with this dude?"

Mona got out of the chair and stood by Terrance, looping her arm through his. "Yes. Terrance and I are here on a date."

"Mona, he could never love you like I do."

Terrance intervened. "She told you we're on a date and you're interrupting it, so can you please leave us alone?"

Mona could tell that things were about to get heated. In order to defuse the situation, she jumped in. "Garrett, I'll talk to you later. Now can you please honor our wishes and leave us be?"

Garrett popped his collar. "Fine." He walked away with a scowl on his face.

"Can you believe that dude? I came *this* close"—Terrance held his thumb and forefinger together—"from punching him out."

Mona grabbed his hand. "I'm glad you didn't. Where's my drink?"

Terrance handed it to her. She took a sip and savored each drop. It was a Cosmopolitan, and it was fixed just right. The situation could have exploded into something more, she thought as she exhaled.

After they finished their drinks, Mona was ready to get back on the dance floor. She and Terrance moved through the crowd. The deejay played back-to-back songs by a popular hip-hop artist. By the time the music marathon was over, they were drenched in sweat. They headed straight to the bar.

Terrance handed Mona a napkin. "Let me go to the ladies' room. I'll meet you back here," she said.

Terrance wiped the sweat from his face. "Okay, babes."

Mona went to the bathroom and used a wet paper towel to wipe her face. She reapplied some of her makeup before exiting.

As she was leaving, she bumped straight into Garrett.

"Whoa," he said, catching her before she could trip.

"Thanks," she said, and began to walk away.

Garrett grabbed her by the arm, stopping her.

"I know the glitz and glamour can be enticing, but men in that world don't know how to be faithful. I don't want you to get hurt."

Mona jerked her arm away. She got close to him because she didn't want to cause a scene. "Don't *ever* grab me like that again. Who I see is my business. I loved you at one time, yes. Could it have worked out? Maybe, but I've moved on. For the *last time*, you need to move on too."

"I have. I just want you to know that when he hurts you, I'm here."

Garrett walked away without saying anything else.

Mona smoothed her dress, then walked back to the bar and located Terrance.

He leaned in and kissed her on the cheek when she returned. He handed her a drink. It didn't take her long to drink the apple martini.

"Do you want another one?" he asked.

She saw Garrett staring from across the room. She turned her back on him. "Yes. One for the road."

Chapter Forty-Seven

THE NEXT FEW DAYS FLEW by. Mona and Terrance got reacquainted with one another and back into their normal routine. She handed him his morning coffee. He placed it on the desk in front of him.

"Our new assistant will be here shortly."

Mona sat on Terrance's lap. "Oh, she's *ours* now?" he asked.

"Yes. She will be working for you and me. That way I can keep an eye on her. I know how easy it is to get a crush on a boss. Especially one that's as handsome as you."

"You must be working on a raise."

"If what I feel poking at me is any indication, I think I already did." Mona kissed him.

The door opened.

Terrance moaned. "Dang. We got company. I knew I should have told you to lock the door."

Mona stood and straightened her skirt. "I'll take care of this. You take care of that." She pointed at the erection tenting his pants.

He shifted in his seat and tried to think of something to get his erection to disappear.

The sound of his cell phone with his mom's special ringtone playing did the trick. He'd been avoiding her calls for the last two days. He answered because he didn't need her dropping by.

"Yes, Mom."

"That is not the proper way to answer your phone. I know I raised you better," Sara snapped.

"Mom, what is it? I don't have time to argue with you."

"I just wanted to see how you were doing. I miss our daily talks."

"I told you if you were going to be saying anything negative about Mona that we would have to keep our distance."

"You're going to allow some woman to come between us?" Sara asked.

"Mom. You'll always be my mother. But Mona is my woman."

"Are you sure about that? What about the good doctor?" Sara asked.

"I have to go." Terrance ended the call in the middle of their conversation.

He didn't want to think about Garrett and Mona together, but his mom did have a point. Mona needed to make a decision, and Terrance hoped, for his sake, that she chose him.

They left the office, stopping by Mona's house so she could pack some clothes, and then they drove to his place.

Once they were inside, Terrance convinced her to take a shower with him. They took turns washing each other's backs. The hot, soapy water flowed down Mona's back. Terrance planted kisses following the trail. He kissed the softness of her buttocks. He turned her around to face him. While on his knees, he took her into his mouth and pleasured her until she climaxed.

He needed to be inside of her. She leaned against the shower wall. Terrance stood behind her and entered her from behind. Their bodies rocked in unison as they held on to the wall for support. Terrance kissed the back of Mona's neck. The intensity of his desire increased as he called out her name, feeling pure ecstasy.

Once out of the shower, they got in his bed and watched classic movies until they both drifted off to sleep. The next day, Terrance prepared breakfast in bed. He frowned when he heard Mona in a heated phone discussion. She wasn't curled under the covers like he's left her. Instead, her legs were dangling to the side as she spoke on her phone.

Terrance carried the tray and set it next to her on the bed. She ended her conversation. "Baby, you didn't have to make breakfast. You should have woken me. I could have cooked."

Terrance ignored her comment and said, "Who was that on the phone?"

"My sister. Her call is what woke me. I decided to stop avoiding her."

"Sounds like you two were arguing."

"We were. But we got things straight now. Everything is okay."

"Are you sure?" Terrance asked. "Because I can tell you're tense by the sound of your voice."

"Feed me and I'll be all better."

They took turns feeding each other fruit. Terrance dipped the last strawberry in whipped cream. He put one end of the strawberry in his mouth and the other end with the whipped cream in Mona's. They ate until their lips touched. Terrance dipped his tongue in and out of Mona's mouth.

It was a Saturday morning, and neither had plans. They spent the majority of the day cuddled in bed watching and critiquing movies on TV.

It was around four in the afternoon, and neither had put on any clothes, when the doorbell rang. Terrance went and looked out the window. He didn't recognize the silver Range Rover parked near Mona's car.

"Let me go see who this is. I'll be right back."

Terrance put on some boxers and a pair of jogging pants. Then he grabbed a white t-shirt and put it on as he was walking down the stairs.

The doorbell rang again. Terrance looked out the peephole. His mom and Reverend Hamilton stood on the other side. He unlocked the door and opened it.

"Mama. Reverend Hamilton," Terrance said.

"I've been calling you all day," Sara said. "William and I were out, so we decided to stop by. This thing between us has gone on too long, so I'm here in peace."

Terrance didn't like beefing with his mom and wanted to make amends, but now was not the time.

"You shouldn't have dropped by without speaking with me first. I could have been out of town or something," Terrance said.

"Have you eaten? If not, get dressed. William and I can treat you to dinner."

"I'm fine."

Sara started walking toward the living room with Reverend Hamilton right behind her. Terrance had no choice but to follow.

"Your house always looks clean when I come by. I'm glad of that," Sara said on the way to the living room.

"Mom, I have a cleaning service come in once a week, so it should."

"Nice house you have here, son," Reverend Hamilton added.

"Thanks. Mom helped me with the decorations." Terrance hoped his giving her props would ease the tension between the two of them.

Sara and Reverend Hamilton sat on the sofa.

Terrance needed to figure out his next move. Should he appease his mom on the sofa or go check on Mona in his bed?

Chapter Forty-Eight

IT WAS TAKING TERRANCE TOO long to come back up the stairs. Curiosity got the best of Mona, so she sent him a text. She heard his phone beep. His phone was still on the nightstand.

Not wanting to wait much longer for him to return, Mona got out of bed, went to the closet, and removed her overnight bag. She retrieved a pair of jeans and a shirt. She wasn't concerned about ironing them at this point. Instead, she found a hair tie and pulled her hair back in a ponytail.

She slipped on a pair of flats and headed down the stairs. She ran right into Terrance.

"Baby, I was coming back."

"Who was at the door?" Mona asked.

"Ugh, nobody."

"If it was nobody, why are you looking over your shoulder?"

"Well, what happened was…" Terrance started. He tried to lead her back upstairs. Mona wouldn't budge.

"Terrance, if you don't tell me who was at the door, you and I are going to have some problems." Mona didn't blink. She placed her hand on her hip and tilted her head to the side.

"It's my mom."

"Your mom."

Terrance tried to hush her.

"What is *she* doing here?" Mona asked.

"She's here with her fiancé. They're in the living room."

"I don't feel like seeing her. Can't you get rid of her?"

"I tried. She insists on us talking."

"Maybe I should leave. I'm in a peaceful place and don't feel like any drama." Mona turned around.

Terrance grabbed her arm. "No, don't go. We planned on spending the weekend together. My mom being here doesn't change that."

"I'll be upstairs." She removed his hand from her arm and headed back to his room.

Terrance followed behind her. "I think the only way to resolve things with my mother is to have you there by my side. She needs to see us together. You're important to me. And she's important to me."

Mona paused on the stairway. "Fine. But I'm telling you now, if she starts getting disrespectful, you need to stop her. I shouldn't have to say anything to her because she's your mom, not mine."

"Understood. Now, can we turn your frown into a smile?" he asked.

She continued to pout. "I'll think about it."

"Pleeease?" Terrance began tickling her.

Mona couldn't control herself and started laughing.

He laughed too. "That's more like it."

She followed him to the living room, taking a few deep breaths before entering.

Sara and Reverend Hamilton were talking but stopped when they entered.

Reverend Hamilton stood and shook Mona's hand. Sara looked away and acted like she wasn't there.

"Hello, Sara."

Sara looked at Mona with venom in her eyes. "It's *Mrs. Beckham*. Didn't your parents teach you some manners?"

"Yes. They taught me to respect those who respect me."

Terrance tugged on Mona's arm. "Let's sit."

Mona sat in the love seat next to Terrance.

The tension between the two women could be cut with a knife.

Terrance cleared his throat. "Would anyone like something to drink?" he asked, looking from one person to the next.

"Nothing for me," Sara responded.

"I'm fine." Mona crossed her arms and leaned back in the chair.

Reverend Hamilton said, "I'll take a glass of juice, if you have any."

"I sure do. Mona, do you want to help me out in the kitchen?"

Mona didn't look at Terrance. "Why don't you show the reverend around while you get his drink? Your mom and I will be *just fine.*"

Terrance looked as if he didn't want to. He stood silently longer than he should have but eventually said, "Come on, reverend."

Mona watched them leave. Sara held a magazine and pretended to be looking at it. Mona laughed because the magazine was upside down, so she knew she wasn't really reading it.

"Sara—I mean, Mrs. Beckham… I'm glad we're alone so we can talk. Woman to woman."

Sara grunted but didn't say anything.

"You don't have to speak, just listen. I love your son. Your son loves me. I will never do anything to hurt Terrance. He means the world to me, and I plan to show him each and every day. You've raised an amazing man."

Sara threw the magazine on the table. "You don't have to tell me about my son. I know everything there is to know about him. What I don't know is *you.* Who are your people? Why were you working as his assistant? If you're so intelligent and independent, you wouldn't need Terrance."

Mona shifted in her seat. She clenched her hands near her side and exhaled before responding. "You want to know who my people are? Well, let me tell you. I come from a family of hard workers. My father worked two jobs to support his family. My mom was a stay-at-home mother who took care of her three children and husband. My family's not poor, but neither are they rich. My parents made sure we lived in a stable home and we had all the love and care we needed. I could have easily stayed in Texas and gone to a college there, but because I've always had the desire to be a screenwriter, I decided to attend the University of California and got a full scholarship because of my 4.0 grade point average."

Sara seemed to be on information overload. She held her hand out as if motioning to stop Mona. "Fine. I misjudged you, but I still don't know if you're the right person for my son."

"Shouldn't Terrance be the one to decide if I'm right for him? I understand he's your son, but he's not a little boy anymore. He's a grown man and more than capable of making his own decisions."

Terrance and the reverend returned to the room. Terrance asked, "You two all right?"

"We're fine," Mona said. She looked at Sara, and Sara looked at her.

Chapter Forty-Nine

TERRANCE LOOKED AT EACH WOMAN. Mona seemed fine. His mother seemed anxious. She kept fidgeting with his magazine.

"Sara, Terrance told me I could come sit on set with him one day," Reverend Hamilton said. "That'll be exciting. I've always wanted to see how movies were made."

Sara avoided eye contact. "That's good, dear. I'm sure you'll enjoy yourself."

"He also shared with me that Ms. Mona here wrote this screenplay, and one of the networks has commissioned our boy." Reverend Hamilton looked at Terrance. "Yes, son, I consider you my boy." He then looked at Sara and continued, "Terrance will be producing the show and Mona will be the head writer, since it's her idea."

Sara looked at Mona. "So have you got everything you've dreamed of?"

"Yes, ma'am. I'm not going to take all of the credit. Terrance and my friend Charlotte presented the idea to the network, so if it wasn't for those two, I would still be searching for someone to produce my stuff. The beauty of it all is that Terrance"—Mona squeezed his hand—"and I will be working together."

"When were you going to tell me?" Sara asked her son. "I heard about the deal on TV."

"Mom, you should know by now that I try to keep my business and personal lives separate."

Sara glared at Mona. "I can't tell."

"Don't go there," Terrance said.

Mona interjected, "Terrance, your mom has a point. Our lives *have* intermingled. We are in a relationship and we're working together. So as hard as you've tried to keep it separate, it's a mix."

He chuckled. "I guess it is. Mom, I stand corrected. Now that you know, I hope you will stop tripping about Mona."

"Mona and I have come to an understanding," Sara said. She looked at Mona. "Haven't we?"

Mona smiled. "Yes, we have."

Terrance sighed. "Good. Now, why don't Mona and I go change, and then I will treat you and Reverend Hamilton to dinner."

"Dear, can we get a rain check? And as far as Sunday dinner, some of the members are taking us out to eat, so we'll have to cancel."

"No problem. I'm sure Mona and I can handle our own Sunday dinner," Terrance assured her.

Sara stood. "Well, son, thanks for your hospitality, but we should be going. I want to beat the traffic," Reverend Hamilton said.

"The next time you want to come this way, let me send a ride for you," Terrance suggested.

"No. That's a waste of money," Sara said.

"Mom. I can't take it with me, so I might as well spend it on someone I love."

He hugged Sara.

"Enjoy the rest of your day," Mona said, standing.

"You too," Sara responded.

Terrance and Mona walked his mom and the reverend to the front door. Sara hugged Terrance and whispered, "I love you."

"I love you too, Mom."

She kissed him on the cheek and walked out. The reverend shook Terrance's hand. "Take care."

Terrance wrapped his arm around Mona's waist and watched them get in the car. He waited until they pulled away before closing the door.

He turned Mona toward him. "What did you say to her to change her attitude?"

"Let's just say she understands that I love you and I'm not going anywhere anytime soon."

"I'm glad to hear it. Which leaves me to ask, when do you want to leave to see your parents?"

"I still haven't decided if I want to go."

"Come on, baby. I'm sure you miss your family. Besides, if we're going to be together, your folks need to meet the man their daughter is crazy about."

"I said I love you. Never said I was *crazy* about you," she teased.

"You don't have to say it. I know these things. Now, where were we before we got interrupted?"

Terrance gathered Mona in his arms, carried her to his room, and laid her on the bed. They started off with a kiss and ended with their naked bodies entwined under the covers.

Chapter Fifty

MONA WATCHED TERRANCE SLEEP. SHE turned and looked out the window of the 747 jet. The white clouds looked like cotton. She eased her seat back and closed her eyes. After the long week they'd had, they deserved a weekend getaway. She'd trained their new assistant and Terrance had worked on finalizing crew members for the show and an upcoming film he was producing.

The pilot's voice came over the speaker. "We're approaching Dallas Fort Worth International Airport. The weather is sunny but you'll need a light jacket. We hope that you've enjoyed your flight. Flight attendants, please prepare for landing. Thank you for flying with us, and we hope you choose us for your next flight."

Mona hit the button on her seat to move it to the upright position. She nudged Terrance. "Wake up, baby. We're about to land."

"Okay," he sleepily responded.

Mona felt excited and nervous all at the same time. She normally flew coach, so she wasn't used to the perks of flying first class, such as being one of the first people off the plane. She held her big handbag while Terrance grabbed their two carry-ons.

"Welcome to my city," she said as they walked through the huge airport.

They went straight to the rental car counter. Terrance rented a sedan, and not long afterward they were placing their items in the back of the Lexus.

"I know you normally drive, but I think this time you should let me." Mona held out her hand for the keys.

"No arguments here." Terrance held open the driver's door. Mona got inside. He handed her the keys, closed the door, and went to sit on the passenger side.

"L.A. traffic is bad, but Dallas traffic is on a whole other level. I might get a little road rage, so please excuse me."

Terrance laughed. "Traffic can't be *that* bad here."

Mona left the airport and got on I-635 headed east. She didn't have a toll tag, so she wanted to avoid the tollway. As they neared North Dallas Parkway, traffic got congested and moved at a snail's pace.

"You've *got* to be kidding me. It's nine in the morning on a Saturday. Shouldn't people be at home sleeping?" Terrance complained.

"You would think. But once I hit the parkway and go north, it's a straight shot. We'll have to go through some lights, but hopefully be out of some of this traffic."

Thirty minutes later, Mona pulled the black car into her old neighborhood in Frisco. She smiled at the memories.

"These are some nice homes," Terrance said.

"My dad worked two jobs to move us from South Dallas to this neighborhood."

"I'm a little nervous about meeting your parents. What if your father doesn't think I'm good enough for his daughter?"

"My dad's not like that. As long as you treat me right, he's happy."

Mona pulled the car in front of the two-car garage. She looked at Terrance. "This was home for me from seventh grade until I graduated high school."

Terrance got out of the car and opened the driver's door for her. She gave him a reassuring hug and kiss right before ringing the doorbell.

"I forgot the bell doesn't work." She knocked r.

Mona's mother opened the door. She had the same height and physique as Mona. She looked like Mona's twin except older, with streaks of gray in her hair, and instead of it being long, she'd cut it to look more like a Halle Berry short style.

Mother and daughter hugged for what seemed like minutes. "My baby's home." She released Mona and acknowledged Terrance. "And is this the young man you were telling me about?"

"Mom, this is Terrance. Terrance, this is my mom."

"Hi, Mrs. Johnson." Terrance extended his hand.

Mona's mom pulled him into an embrace. "We hug around here."

"Yes, ma'am," he responded.

Mona shrugged.

"Come on in," her mother said. "I told Mona that you both are welcome to stay here."

Mona looped her arm through her mom's. "We have a reservation at the Westin, so we won't be far away."

"Your dad's out back. He'll be thrilled to know you're here."

"Is that my baby girl? I thought I heard a car pull up." Mona's dad, who was fit and stood six feet one inches, walked through the kitchen and met them in the living room.

Mona ran over to her dad and hugged him. "Love you, Pops."

"You must be special if my Mona's bringing you home to meet us." Her dad stared at Terrance.

Everyone remained silent. Finally, Mona's father held out his hand. "Welcome, son."

Mona sighed with relief.

Chapter Fifty-One

BEING AROUND MONA'S DAD MADE Terrance yearn for his own father. Her dad made Terrance feel at ease. They immediately bonded over sports. They had a friendly debate on who was the best football team, the Cowboys or the 49ers. They shared a love for the Lakers.

Mona spent a lot of time talking with her mother, so it had given Terrance and her father a lot of time to talk.

"My son and daughter and their families will be over later. I suggest you two go check in to your hotel and relax a little," her dad said. "I'm just getting to know you, but I can tell you're a man with high morals, and the only thing I ask of you is to treat my daughter like I would."

Terrance shook his hand. "I love Mona and will protect her with my life if it ever comes to it."

"Come on. Let's go find our women."

Four hours later, Mona and Terrance were resting in their hotel room.

"Dinner is at six, so don't you think we should be getting ready?" he asked.

Mona snuggled closer to him on the bed. "I don't want to go."

"We're going. Your father is expecting us, and him and I get along great. Just give me the address, because I'm going with or without you." Terrance smiled.

"You would leave me at the hotel by myself?" Mona pouted.

"Your dad told me what your mama was cooking, so I sure would. I'm hungry. I've been saving my appetite all day."

"My sister is still not out of the doghouse with me."

"I thought y'all made up?" Terrance said.

"We did, but I'm not looking forward to seeing her."

Terrance ran his hand gently through her hair. "Baby, whatever happened between the two of you, get over it. I wish I had siblings. You just don't know how lucky you are."

"I guess you're right. I want to take a shower. I want first dibs." She sat up.

"We'll flip for it." Terrance reached to the side of the bed and removed a quarter from his pants pocket. "Heads or tails?"

"Tails."

He flipped the coin in the air and placed it on the back of his hand. He looked at it. It had come up heads. "You're lucky. Don't use up all the hot water."

"I won't." Mona got out of bed and went to the bathroom.

Two hours later, Terrance and Mona stood outside of her parents' home waiting for someone to answer the door. "Do I look all right?" she asked.

"Baby, you look great. I've never seen you not look good," he responded as he admired Mona in her black jeans, cowboy boots, and red button-down shirt. They were actually matching. He'd wanted some cowboy boots, so Mona took him to a store nearby and they both got pairs.

The door opened, and a man Terrance didn't know stood there.

Mona's face brightened with joy. "Justin." They hugged. "Justin, this is Terrance. Terrance, this is my older brother."

"Her only brother." Justin shook Terrance's hand. "Come on. Everybody's waiting on you." He held the door wide open.

They were greeted by Justin's family first. "This is Demetria, my wife."

Terrance shook her hand, then followed Mona as she greeted each family member, introducing him while they walked through the house. "I want you to meet my sister. She's in the kitchen with Mom." She towed him toward the kitchen.

"Danielle, this is Terrance. The new love of my life," Mona said after they hugged each other.

Danielle looked at Terrance. "Not bad. Not bad at all. Welcome to the family. You *are* marrying my sister, aren't you?"

"Danielle! Our plans are none of your business," Mona said.

"I'm only trying to find out his intentions. It's the job of an older sister."

"You don't have to answer her question," Mona told Terrance. "My dad's in the living room. Give me a little time to talk with Danielle and I'll meet you in there shortly."

Terrance could sense the tension between the sisters and exited the kitchen as quickly as he could.

He went to the living room and took a seat on the opposite end of the couch from Justin.

"I knew you would be back," Mona's dad said from his recliner next to the couch.

Justin laughed. "I did too. You see where I am. Right here with Pops, chilling. But let me warn you. Since they're doing the cooking, we will have kitchen duty. I made it easy for us. I bought some paper plates."

They all laughed.

Chapter Fifty-Two

WHILE MONA'S MOTHER MOVED AROUND the kitchen, Danielle's phone rattled against the counter. Mona's eyes flicked to the screen, catching Garrett's name before she looked away. Danielle reentered the kitchen smiling, chatting easily with their mother.

Mona waited for their mother to leave the room before confronting Danielle.

"I glanced at your phone when you left and saw you'd been texting Garrett."

"How dare you invade my privacy?" Danielle said.

"You left your phone on the counter. It was vibrating," Mona snapped.

"Just because things didn't work out with you and Garrett, doesn't mean he and I can't be friends." Danielle placed her phone on the table.

"I couldn't care less about your friendship. But when it comes to me and what I got going on, you have no business discussing it. Why are you telling him I'm in Dallas?"

"He's been whining. I wanted him to know you're serious about this guy so he can move on with his life."

Mona crossed her arms. "Instead of being all in my business, I suggest you handle your own. Where's your husband?"

"He's somewhere. I don't know. He'll be here."

"It's after six and he's not here." Mona hadn't meant to go there with her, but she was tired of Danielle's interfering. Her life was fine without Garrett.

"Look. Like I told you over the phone. Once Garrett shared with me what happened nine years ago, I felt you deserved to know. I remember how depressed you were. I just wanted to give you the closure *I* never got when Scotty broke my heart."

Danielle started crying. Mona remembered how Scotty had left her at the altar without an explanation. She walked around the counter dividing them and placed her arm around Danielle. "Scotty was a jerk. But the man you got now is a good one. You have to stop being verbally abusive to him. If you don't, he's going to find solace somewhere else, and you don't want that, do you?"

"No. I don't. I love Kevin. He's been good to me, and he's a great father," Danielle confessed. She wiped the tears from her face with a paper towel.

"And please stop telling Garrett my business. Because what I'm sure he hasn't told you is that, until recently, he's been a borderline stalker."

Mona shared with Danielle everything that had occurred since she'd been back in contact with Garrett. "So as you can see, I've been clear to him about how I feel. I hate that our relationship ended based on a lie created by his mom, but I'm happy."

"I know you. You've always wanted to be married, but from what I've read about Terrance, he's not the commitment type."

"I want you to get to know Terrance while we're here. You'll see for yourself. He's nothing like you read about online. In Hollywood, you have to put out an image."

"Be careful. I don't want to see you get hurt again."

"I have to thank an online friend, because if it hadn't been for him, I wouldn't be able to see that my perfect match wasn't on the computer—I'd been working with him all along."

Their mother re-entered the kitchen, interrupting their conversation. "Can you ladies help me take these dishes to the table?"

"Sure," they said in unison.

"Glad to see you both can agree to something. You're sisters. I don't want to ever hear of you going more than a day being angry with one another."

"Yes, ma'am." Mona carried a casserole dish of macaroni and cheese and followed her mom to the dining room.

After they filled the table with the food, Danielle gathered everyone into the dining room. Mona's dad said grace and they were seated. Danielle and Demetria fixed the children's plates first. A smaller table stood nearby. Once the kids were seated and began to eat, the adults sat around the larger dining room table.

Mona and Terrance sat next to each other. Mona smiled. She noticed Terrance was getting along with her father and brother. She could tell from the friendly conversation they were having.

Everyone filled their plates with food. Terrance made himself at home. Her mom smiled when she saw him go for seconds.

The doorbell rang.

Justin stopped eating. "I'll get it."

A few minutes later, he returned. Danielle jumped out of her seat. "Baby, you made it."

Kevin said, "I told you I was coming as soon as I got off work."

"I thought… Never mind. Go wash your hands and I'll make you a plate."

"I can fix my own plate," Kevin said.

"No. You've been working hard. I got this."

He smiled. "I'll be back. You know what I like. Pile it on."

Mona caught Danielle's eye, winked at her, and gave her a thumbs-up.

When Kevin returned, Danielle introduced him to Terrance. The rest of the dinner went by with casual conversation. Afterward, the men cleaned and the women went to the living room to relax. Mona sat back in the recliner and closed her eyes. Life right now was good.

Chapter Fifty-Three

TERRANCE GENTLY SHOOK MONA. THEY'D arrived back in Los Angeles on the red-eye. She's slept for the hour and a half it took to get from the airport back to his place. He smiled, remembering the nice weekend he'd enjoyed with her family. He adored her dad and had bonded with her brother. He only wished the trip could have been longer.

Mona yawned and stretched when she woke. "Baby, I'm sorry I fell asleep on you."

"I would have let you sleep, but I don't think I have the energy to carry you *and* the bags inside."

She looked at the dashboard clock. "It's only four in the morning here. I'm going back to sleep as soon as my head hits the pillow."

Less than fifteen minutes later, Mona had done just that. She'd discarded her clothes and gotten under the covers, and Terrance heard her snoring. He placed their bags in the closet, undressed, and got in bed beside her.

The alarm clock woke them both out of their sound sleep. Neither moved to hit the snooze, so the buzz got louder and louder.

Terrance reached over Mona and hit the snooze button.

"Can't we play hooky today?" she asked.

"I wish. I got a meeting with the executives. Correction, *we* got a meeting."

Mona blinked a few times. "I'm awake. I didn't know I needed to be in this meeting."

"You're my **head** writer and my co-producer. Your role has officially changed, so get ready." He scooted to the edge of the bed. "I'm going to take my shower first, and that'll give you a little time to get yourself together."

Two hours later, Terrance and Mona were seated in a conference room at the network with some of the supporting team members Terrance had hired. After the network representative finished welcoming them to the company, Terrance stood in front and officially introduced everyone.

People cheered when Terrance introduced Mona as the head writer. "Without her idea, we wouldn't all be sitting here," he said.

Mona smiled in appreciation while getting his laptop connected to the projector so he could go over the timelines with the team.

"It's ready," she said.

Terrance hit the button on the screen and his presentation began. He went over everyone's responsibilities and expectations for the series. "Please make sure I have all of your updated contact information. We will be emailing the schedule out by the end of this week. Are there any questions or comments?"

He scanned the room and made sure to make eye contact with each person. No one had anything else to add. People with information changes filled out the forms and passed them to Mona. The meeting adjourned. Some lingered to talk with one another. Charles, one of the network executives, walked up to Terrance and Mona. "I'm excited. You two make a great team."

Terrance looked at Mona. "We do, don't we?"

Charles shook Terrance's hand and walked out of the room. Mona turned off the laptop and placed it in the carrying case. "I'm ready when you are. I have a lot of work to do."

"I got the bag." Terrance took the handle from Mona. Their hands touched. He wanted to kiss her but knew it would be unprofessional to do so.

The moment they were in the car, he said, "I need an energy booster."

"We can stop at the convenience store that's about two blocks from here."

"No, you don't understand." Terrance unbuckled his seatbelt, leaned over, and kissed Mona.

The kiss was so intense that she seemed in a daze when he stopped and fell back in his seat.

"Ooh. Now that was a kiss." She licked her lips and smiled.

Terrance drove toward the office. He tuned in to a jazz station and held Mona's hand. They rode in silence, just enjoying each other's company.

Jerricka, the new assistant, met them in the parking lot.

"I hope you got my text before driving over," Mona said.

"I was already on the way, so I just went to the coffee shop and did some work on my thesis until I got your last text informing me you were on your way," Jerricka responded.

"Good. Mona will get you a copy of the office key, so if one of us is not here, you'll be able to open the doors," Terrance assured her as they all walked inside.

"And for your safety, I would suggest if you're by yourself to keep the door locked," Mona added.

Terrance headed to his office and left Mona alone with Jerricka to show her what she needed to do.

The office phone rang. Jerricka's voice came over the intercom. "Mr. Beckham, your mom is on the line."

Terrance lifted the receiver. "Hi, Mom. I was going to call you."

"It's Mona, isn't it? She's keeping you so busy that you don't have time for me," his mother blurted.

"Mom, I'm getting tired of you taking jabs at Mona. If I don't call you, it's because I didn't have time," he said, annoyed.

"I'm sorry. You don't have to be so *harsh*."

"I'm not trying to sound harsh. I just want you to ease up off Mona."

"I'll try."

"We shall see. Look, I got to go. Was there anything else?" Terrance leaned back in his chair.

"No. Just wanted to hear my baby's voice."

"Your baby is fine. I promise. I'll call you later." He ended the call.

Chapter Fifty-Four

MONA'S NEW PROTÉGÉE SEEMED TO be working out well. Mona felt comfortable enough for Jerricka to handle things on her own, and moved the last of her stuff to her new office.

"I have a special delivery." Terrance walked in the room and handed her an envelope.

Mona opened it and saw a check made out for five figures. She blinked. "Oh my. I don't know what to say."

"Baby, there will be plenty more of those."

She wrapped her arms around Terrance's neck. "Thank you for making my dream come true. Because of you, I can add 'screenwriter' to my résumé."

"I'm glad you trusted me with your baby." He kissed her lightly and then used his tongue to gain entry into her mouth.

The sound of Jerricka clearing her throat behind them made them break their embrace.

Mona bit her bottom lip. Terrance wiped the lipstick off his lips.

Jerricka said, "Sorry to interrupt. Mr. Beckham, the person you've been waiting on to call is on the phone."

"Thank you, Jerricka. And for the umpteenth time, call me Terrance. Mr. Beckham was my father."

Terrance left Mona and Jerricka to answer his call.

Mona faced the new assistant. "I'm sure catching Terrance and me kissing isn't a big surprise."

Jerricka smiled. "I knew something was going on. Especially when I saw all of the flowers with the notes lying around signed by him."

Mona blushed. "He's such a romantic."

"I want what you two have one day." Jerricka looked starry-eyed.

"Being with Terrance isn't all easy, and I'll bet you he'll say the same about me." Mona laughed. "Come. I need you to do something for me."

She led Jerricka out of her office, got the stack of papers off the printer, and handed it to Jerricka. "I'll print the envelopes for you. Match the name on the letter with the name on the envelope. When you finish, drop them off to the mailroom down the hall."

"I remember where it is," Jerricka said.

"Great. Give me a minute and you should be able to get the envelopes off the printer. I need to run to the bank. If Terrance asks you where I am, that's where I'll be."

Mona printed off the envelopes for Jerricka right before leaving the office. Mona usually used the drive-through window when handling her bank business, but today, with the size of her check, she decided to park and go inside.

Her palms were sweaty as she filled out the deposit slip. She double-checked the account number she'd written down to make sure she hadn't made a mistake. She didn't want all of her money going into the wrong account.

She handed the bank teller the check. Her eyes widened when she saw the amount. "Ms. Johnson, if there's anything else you need me to do, let me know."

"Depositing the check is all I need right now."

"Any special plans?" the teller asked as she handled the transaction.

"None at the moment." Mona tapped her foot. She didn't have time for small talk. She needed to revise a script so she could email it to her new writing team.

The teller handed Mona the deposit slip. Mona's smile widened when she noticed her healthy account balance.

"When will the funds be available?" she asked.

"We released a thousand to you today, but the rest should clear within the next two to three business days."

"Thank you. Have a good day," Mona told the teller before practically skipping out of the bank with joy.

Before pulling out of the parking lot, she sent Charlotte and Kem a text message asking them both to meet her at the bar so she could treat them to a few drinks. She wanted to celebrate with her two best friends.

Jerricka wasn't in the office when Mona returned. According to her note, she'd left to go take the mail. Mona smiled and went to Terrance's office.

"Jerricka told me you'd gone to the bank," he said when she entered.

"Yes. Next stop will be me looking for a bigger place. I'm just waiting for the check to clear."

"I've been meaning to talk to you about your living situation. Why don't you move in with me?"

Mona thought about it. She did already spend a lot of time at his place. "Let me think about it."

Terrance batted his eyelashes. "Pleeeease. I'll make space for you in my closet. You can redecorate if you want. Tell me what I need to do to convince you to move in and I'll do it."

Mona raised her hand, twisted it from side to side, and sang the chorus of Beyoncé's "Single Ladies."

"I have no problems doing that. Just give me a little time."

Mona stopped doing her little hand dance. She was kidding, but Terrance wasn't.

Chapter Fifty-Five

TERRANCE LEFT THE OFFICE AND went straight to a local jeweler his family liked to use. Mona didn't think he was serious about marriage, but he needed her to realize the depths of his love for her. He loved her more than any other woman he'd ever met. She completed him. She complemented him in all areas. He would be a fool to let her slip through his hands. He wanted to hold her every night. He wanted to make sure she was safe and secure, and would do whatever it took to get her to understand that by his side was where she belonged. If putting a ring on it would convince her to move in with him, then so be it.

Terrance described to the jeweler his idea of a perfect ring. The jeweler returned and showed him several. Terrance wasn't expecting to hear two recognizable voices come in.

"William didn't tell me you were going to be here too," Sara said.

"Too?" Terrance was dumbfounded.

Sara stood next to him and picked out one of the bridal ring sets. She looked at Reverend Hamilton. "Are you sure you can afford this on your budget?"

"Reverend Hamilton isn't trying to buy one of these—I am, Mother."

Sara's mouth fell open so wide a horsefly could have flown inside. "It's too early for you to be thinking about marrying that woman."

"Mom, I'm a grown man. I decide when I'm ready. And that woman has a name."

"I know her name. Just because we're getting along, doesn't mean I want you to marry her."

"It's not your choice."

Reverend Hamilton reached for her hand. "Dear, we came to pick out your ring. Let's not spoil it with your temper tantrum over Terrance's girlfriend."

"Looks like she's about to be his fiancée. There's no way she's going to turn him down when he presents one of those to her," she said.

"When do you plan on popping the question, son?"

"Not sure," Terrance replied. "But soon, because she's talking about finding a new place, and I want her to move in with me."

Sara interjected, "I don't agree with shacking up, but in this case I would make an exception. Live with her first. You can think about marrying her later."

"Sara, I'm shocked. Your son is trying to do the right thing and you're encouraging him to sin." Reverend Hamilton dropped her hand.

"But dear… You said yourself that kids today rush into things. All I want him to do is slow down and make sure Mona is the woman he wants. He hasn't explored all of his options."

"I'm sure these folks are tired of hearing our business, so I've decided what ring I want and you two can finish the business you came here for," he replied.

Terrance looked at the jeweler. "I like this one. She wears a size seven. When will it be ready?"

The jeweler smiled. "Good choice. I can have it ready by Friday. Do you want to come by or have me special deliver it?"

"I'll have it delivered."

"Just fill this out and we'll get this transaction completed." The jeweler handed Terrance an iPad and a stylus.

"I can't believe you're spending that much money on a ring. Son, I didn't raise you to be wasteful," Sara said.

"No, you didn't. Dad raised me to make sure I was protected and invested, and I'm investing in my future. Mona's my future whether you like it or not."

Sara pouted.

Reverend Hamilton said, "I don't feel like looking at rings. Let's go, Sara."

"William, what do you mean? The wedding is in a few weeks, and we need the rings."

"I need to think about some things," he said, and walked away.

"Mom, I suggest you try to handle your own personal business before trying to get involved in mine," Terrance said once the reverend had left the store.

"William's just pouting. He'll be all right."

He looked at his mom as if she were crazy. "Did you not hear what he said? He said he needs to think over some things, which translates to him having second thoughts on marrying you."

"He wouldn't break things off with me. I'm a good catch."

Terrance wrapped his arm around his mom's shoulders. "Yes, you are. But right now, you've made the reverend upset, so instead of talking to me, you better go catch him, because I don't have plans to drive all the way to Pasadena."

Sara stormed away in a huff. Terrance laughed. The good reverend was giving his mom a tough dose of love. He knew Reverend Hamilton was upset, but not crazy enough to leave his mother stranded.

Her behavior was getting out of hand. Terrance needed to figure out a way to stop her from meddling in his life. Mona wasn't going anywhere, so the two would have to learn to coexist.

Chapter Fifty-Six

MONA SAT AT THE BAR at the Flamingo Lounge waiting for her friends to appear. She was on her second drink when she received back-to-back texts from each informing her they wouldn't be able to make it.

Mona waved her hand to get the bartender's attention.

"I want to pay my tab," she said.

"Pretty lady, your tab's being taken care of by the gentleman there." He pointed to the end of the bar.

Mona frowned. "Thanks."

She got off the barstool and walked to the end of the bar. "Garrett, if I didn't know any better, I would think you were stalking me."

"My hotel is right across the street. Or did you forget that when you decided to come here?" Garrett said with a smug look on his face.

No, she hadn't been thinking of Garrett when she asked Charlotte and Kem to meet her here. "This time, we'll chalk it up as coincidence."

She turned to walk away. Garrett stood in front of her and blocked her. "Why leave so soon? You just got here."

"My friends stood me up. I don't like to drink alone."

"I don't see why two old friends can't have a drink or two together."

Mona thought about it. Having a drink with Garrett wouldn't harm her. "I see a table over there. It's near the door, so if you try something, I can slip out."

"Still a tease, I see, Ms. Mona Johnson."

"Never that," she responded.

"Do you want another apple martini?" he asked.

"A Cosmo. But let me finish this one first." Mona sipped on her apple martini.

"So how was your trip home?"

"Great. But I'm sure Danielle gave you the rundown."

"I want to apologize to you if it seems like I was crossing the line by talking to her. I went to her because I was hoping she could convince you to give me another chance."

"We're two different people now. I still think you're a wonderful guy, just not the guy for me."

"I understand." Garrett reached for her hand and squeezed it. "Are you ready for that other drink now?"

"I sure am. But where's the waiter? I haven't seen one come by the table."

"I'll get it. Just promise me you'll be here when I return."

"I'm not going anywhere." Mona texted Terrance while waiting for Garrett to return but didn't get a reply. She slipped the phone back in her clutch.

Garrett returned to the table holding two drinks. He placed one in front of Mona and the other on the table near him. "So how are things with you and the producer?"

"Let's not talk about Terrance." Mona took a sip of her drink. She smacked her lips. "Something's not right with this drink."

She took another sip. Her vision started to blur. "Garrett, did you do something to my drink?"

"I don't know what you're talking about."

Mona felt herself feeling lightheaded. Garrett helped her off the stool, wrapping his arm around her as if they were a couple. "I'll help you to your car."

"No, call me a cab."

"Why don't you come to my room and sleep it off? You probably had one too many drinks."

"No, it's something else. I feel funny."

Garrett hugged her and walked her out. Instead of taking her to her car, he walked her toward his hotel. Mona thought she heard someone call out her name. She opened her mouth to respond, but nothing came out.

"Why are we at your hotel?" she asked.

"You're in no condition to drive. Let the drinks wear off and then I'll allow you to leave."

Mona gained the strength she needed and grabbed her clutch from him. "I'm not going anywhere with you," she slurred.

"Come on, Mona. You're causing a scene." He tried to keep a grip on her shoulder, but she shimmied herself from his reach.

"Taxi," she yelled. "Will someone get me a taxi?"

Garrett placed his hand over her mouth. She tried to knock it away, but each time she did, the hand returned.

A tall, slender hotel security guard rounded the corner and asked, "Is everything okay here?"

"Things are fine. She just had a little too much to drink," Garrett responded.

"Find me a taxi," Mona slurred.

"Nonsense. She can stay with me," Garrett insisted.

"Somebody get me a taxiii!" Mona shouted.

The security guard had a confused look on his face. He looked at Garrett. "She wants a taxi, sir. It's in your best interest to follow her wishes."

Garrett moved away. Mona walked back through the hotel lobby like a drunken woman. The security guard hailed her a cab.

"What's your address?" he asked.

"It's on my license." Mona's hand felt heavy.

The security guard took her clutch and located her license, then recited the address to the driver and made sure she was securely in the back of the cab.

He told the driver, "Make sure she gets inside of her place safely."

Mona noticed the guard give the cab driver money. She leaned back and drifted in and out of consciousness.

The cab driver assisted her to the front door. "Thank you. You're so kind. How can I repay you?"

"Your fare's already been taken care of."

"Thank you so much."

"Lock the door. I don't want anything to happen to you."

"It won't. Thanks to yoooou," Mona slurred.

The cab driver gently shoved her inside her apartment, then closed the door. Mona engaged the bottom lock. She lifted her arm to do the same to the top lock but couldn't. Frustrated, she hit the lock with her hand. She didn't feel any pain.

She stumbled through the apartment in the dark, hitting furniture. She fell on the couch facedown and blacked out.

Chapter Fifty-Seven

TERRANCE BLINKED SEVERAL TIMES. HE'D been driving and was going to stop at the Flamingo Lounge to meet Mona after he saw her text. He couldn't believe she was there huddled with Garrett, a man she'd sworn she was through with. Why would she even invite him there if she wanted Garrett? Was it her way of ending things with him? Was it the real reason why she didn't want to move in with him?

How could he have been so foolish? He'd played the game to win Mona's heart and he'd lost. Garrett had come out the victor.

Terrance needed a drink more than ever, but he wouldn't do it at the lounge. He would go home to drown his sorrows.

How could you, Mona? Terrance asked over and over in his head. Instead of drinking, he went to his home gym, deciding to work out his frustrations in another manner. He pushed himself to the maximum doing different exercises.

Sweaty and dehydrated, he went to the kitchen and gulped down a liter of water. He looked at his cell phone and noticed he had a missed call from Mona. Curious what she had to say, he brought up the voicemail.

"We need to talk." She was slurring.

"There's nothing else you can say to me right now," Terrance said out loud.

He threw the phone on his bed, removed his clothes, and got in a hot shower. Every time he closed his eyes he couldn't get the image of Garrett and Mona hugging and walking toward the hotel.

Terrance dried off and got under the covers. He tossed and turned throughout the night. He saw visions of Garrett and Mona kissing and making love in his dreams. He made himself wake up. His dream seemed too real.

He called Mona's cell. His calls went straight to voicemail. She'd turned off her phone. He threw his phone across the bed. It almost landed on the floor. He fell back on the bed and stared at the ceiling until he fell asleep.

The next morning, Terrance went into his office wearing his dark shades to hide the bloodshot eyes he had from lack of sleep.

Jerricka greeted him at the door. He didn't smell fresh coffee like he normally did.

"Good morning, Terrance," she said.

"It's Mr. Beckham."

"But…" Jerricka started, but stopped herself.

"Is Ms. Johnson here yet?" Terrance asked.

"No. She called. She didn't sound too good. She said she wasn't feeling well but will check back in with me later."

Terrance figured she was too hungover after a night with Garrett to come in. "Did she leave a message for me?"

"No, sir. She didn't."

"Let me know if you hear from her. Screen all of my calls. I will be unavailable all day."

"What if your mom calls?"

"Tell her to leave a message." Terrance went to his office and shut the door.

He stared at Mona's picture on his phone. He loved her, but she'd made her decision. She'd chosen Garrett. Terrance needed to get over it and move on. It was simple in theory but hard to execute. Love wasn't an emotion he could erase right away. It'd taken him years to fall in love, and it would take a lifetime to remove Mona from his heart.

He didn't like thinking of defeat, but his eyes had shown him what his heart didn't want to accept. She couldn't let go of her past, so he would have to let *her* go.

Terrance's phone rang. Mona's face flashed on the screen. He answered, "Hello."

"Thank God you answered. I've been calling you all morning."

"What about last night? I called you but you didn't answer."

"About last night—"

"No need to explain. I got another call coming in."

He didn't want to hear Mona lie to him. Cutting her off before she could finish her statement felt like the best thing to do.

Terrance turned on the radio, and Tina Turner's "What's Love Got to Do with It?" came through the speakers.

At this point, love didn't mean a thing. He began questioning everything Mona had said to him. Despite his anger, he loved her. He'd hoped that building a home with her would seal the bond they'd created. But their new memories wouldn't stand a chance against the ones she shared with Garrett.

Terrance felt his heart breaking in two. It caused him to wail.

Jerricka rushed to the door. "Mr. Beckham, are you all right?"

"No, but I will be."

Chapter Fifty-Eight

MONA WOKE WITH HER HEAD feeling like a ton of bricks weighed it down. Every time she sat up, she fell back on the couch. She called Kem and Charlotte. Neither liked the way she sounded and vowed to be over as soon as possible.

Mona's call to Terrance didn't go the way she'd wanted. He'd acted upset with her about something. She didn't know what she'd said to him the night before but hoped he would forgive her.

She barely remembered the chain of events, but things were slowly coming back to her. Mona scrolled through her phone and made a call.

"Garrett, what the hell did you do to me last night?" she shouted.

"What are you talking about?" he asked nonchalantly.

"You know exactly what I'm talking about. Don't try to play stupid with me. You *drugged* me. You thought you were going to take me to your room and take advantage of me, but you didn't count on me not drinking the whole thing."

"Mona, apparently you don't need to drink, because your accusations are ludicrous."

"How could you do this to someone you claimed to love? I used to love you, but I can honestly say that I hate the day I laid eyes on you."

"Let me explain—"

"I don't want to hear anything you have to say." Mona ended the call. Tears flowed down her face. She didn't want to imagine what would have happened if she hadn't fought the urge to give in to the drug he'd slipped in her drink.

Garrett was the last person she'd thought she would have to protect herself from. If her suspicions were true, he would pay for what he'd tried to do to her.

Shortly thereafter, she heard a knock on the door. Kem and Charlotte were standing on the other side.

They all hugged each other.

"You look like crap," Charlotte said.

"I feel like I look." Mona led them to the sofa.

"I love your place," Kem said.

"Don't lie. You're just trying to make me feel better," Mona replied.

"It's small, but it's cute and cozy. Sometimes I wonder why I got such a big house," Kem said.

Mona felt at ease and recounted what had happened the previous night at the bar.

"I feel bad about not being able to come," Charlotte said.

"It's not your fault. It's that jerk Garrett's."

"I knew he was bad news." Kem clenched her fists.

"I need to figure out my next move." Mona looked at the floor.

"Let me make a call." Charlotte pulled out her phone and walked to the other side of the room.

"How are you *really* doing?" Kem asked Mona.

"My head still hurts, but otherwise, I'm fine."

"What did Terrance say?"

"I haven't told him. I tried to tell him over the phone, but he was too busy to talk."

"A guardian angel must have been watching over you. All the right people at the right time were there to help you get from the lounge to your house without incident."

"I thank God for it. Complete strangers tried to protect me while the one I'd trusted tried to ruin me. If he'd been successful, you know how horrible I would have felt." The thought of it made Mona extremely upset.

Kem placed her arm around her. "You're all right now. Nobody's going to hurt you."

They rocked from side to side.

Charlotte ended her call and returned to them. "My friend says you should file a police report. We also need to get you to the doctor so they can take a sample just in case the drugs are still in your system." She went into full PR mode. She hadn't built a successful management firm without having a take-charge attitude.

Mona changed into a pair of jeans and a t-shirt, then met Charlotte's cop friend at the hospital, where he took her statement. A doctor ordered some blood and urine tests.

Charlotte and Kem both ignored their work in order to stay with her. The doctor called them to the back when the test results returned. Another police officer was also in the room.

The doctor handed Mona the results. "So I was drugged?" she asked after looking at the report.

"Your blood had traces of GHB, gamma hydroxybutyric acid, which is a common date-rape drug."

"I knew it. I knew something wasn't right about that drink—that's why I didn't drink all of it."

"You're one of the lucky ones. If you'd drunk the whole thing, I doubt if you would be able to recall much of anything."

The police officer said, "Would you like to press charges?"

"Yes. I don't want him doing this to any other woman. I want Garrett arrested for attempted rape."

The police officer replied in a calm voice, "Based on what we have, unfortunately, we won't be able to charge him with attempted rape."

"What do you mean? He drugged me, and we all know what could have happened if he'd gotten me to his hotel room."

"I'm only telling you this so you won't be disappointed. If we can trace the drug back to him, then we can get him on drugging you."

Charlotte interrupted him. "I smell a cover-up already, and he hasn't even been charged yet."

"Ladies, I can assure you I will do whatever I can to make sure he pays for what he's done to Ms. Johnson."

"Please do. Come on, Mona. Let's go." Charlotte wrapped her arm around Mona's shoulders and led her out.

Chapter Fifty-Nine

IT'D BEEN TWO DAYS SINCE Terrance had seen Mona. She hadn't been in the office, and they hadn't spoken after their last conversation. He'd been tempted to call her several times, but the flashback of seeing Garrett's arm draped around her stopped him. She'd made her choice. Terrance, as much as he hated to, needed to figure out a way to cope.

If she didn't come in today, he would have no choice but to call her. She needed to email out the schedule to the team. He didn't know how to do it, and Jerricka was too new for him to trust her with it.

"Mona, where are you?" he said out loud.

Terrance heard the chime letting him know someone had entered the office. He heard voices. A few moments later, his mom entered holding a basket.

"I came to make peace." Sara walked to his desk and placed the basket in front of him.

"Hi, Mom. We're good."

"You sure? You haven't been saying much since the jewelry-store incident."

"A lot has happened since then."

Sara opened the basket and removed plates of food. "Let's eat and talk."

Up until this point, Terrance hadn't had much of an appetite, but the smell of the shrimp po'boy and pasta salad made his stomach grumble. To top it off, his mom had brought a huge slice of her homemade lemon pound cake.

"I wasn't sure if you had anything to drink, so I brought you some lemon tea." She got out a thirty-two-ounce cup and set it near his plate.

Terrance ate his food as if he were starving. He listened to his mom talk while he ate.

"William and I have worked out our differences, so we will still be getting married."

"I'm glad things worked out for you." Terrance wiped his mouth with a napkin.

"So when do *you* plan on popping the question?" Sara leaned closer to the desk.

"All that's been put on hold for now. I'm not sure I'm the one Mona wants," Terrance confessed.

"She may not be my choice for you, but I'm sure she knows that she will never do any better than you."

"Apparently, she *doesn't* realize it. Her ex is a doctor, and he's been pursuing her. I think he's won her over."

"Ludicrous. After the stink she made, and she picks him over you? Well, dear, one way to get over one woman is to find another one, and I know the perfect replacement."

"Mom, I'm not sure that's the route I want to take. Let me deal with this situation before I step back out in the dating world."

"Nonsense. Elle is around your age. She's the branch manager at the bank I go to. She's single and has a great sense of humor. She'd be perfect."

Terrance didn't have a desire to be with any other woman but Mona. His heart was breaking. He hadn't slept well the last few nights.

But he needed to do *something*. Maybe his mother was right. Maybe going out with Elle would help him move on faster.

"Mom, you're absolutely right. It's time for me to move on. I think going out with Elle is a great idea."

The moment he said those words, he felt his heart tug. Mona stood outside of the door staring at him with not only anger but pain in her eyes. Tears flowed down her cheeks. She turned and walked away.

"Mona!" he called out.

"Let her go. She made her choice. Now you're making yours. Let her go, son."

Terrance looked at his mom and then at the empty space in the doorway.

Sara was right. Mona had chosen Garrett. She was moving on, and now so was he.

Terrance barely heard what else his mom said while she was there. He hugged and kissed her on the cheek after he walked her to the door.

When she was gone, he turned to Jerricka. "Is Mona in her office?"

"No. She wanted me to let you know she's emailed the schedule out. She decided to work from home the rest of the day."

"Finish what you're working on and you can leave yourself. I'll pay you for a full eight hours."

"Thanks, Mr. Beckham." Jerricka smiled.

Terrance walked to his office but stopped when he heard Jerricka call his name.

"Yes?" he said, turning around.

"Mona didn't seem like her normal self. You might want to check on her."

"Mona will be fine. I assure you."

He turned around and walked into his office, shutting the door for privacy. He called his mother. "Mom, cancel the date with Elle.

You've taught me to do the right thing. It wouldn't be fair to her for me to start dating her when I'm still in love with another woman."

"Son, your dad would be proud of the man you've become," she said.

"Thanks. In the meantime, I'm going to forget women and pour myself into my work. I have a show to do, and I'm going for the Emmy."

"Now that's my boy. Love you."

"Love you too, Mom."

Terrance smiled for the first time in days.

Chapter Sixty

MONA ATE THE LAST SCOOP of chocolate chip ice cream. The last few days had been the worst of her life. Her first love had drugged her with intent to assault her, and she'd heard the man she loved make plans to move on and go out with some other woman.

If Sara had been the one to tell Mona, she wouldn't have believed her, would have thought the old woman was just being mean and vindictive, but she'd heard Terrance say it himself. If what she heard was a mistake then Terrance would have come after her, but he hadn't. Instead, he'd stayed in the office with his mom.

Hurt by the chain of events, Mona couldn't stand to be in the office, so she'd stopped by the convenience store on the way home and bought her favorite junk food.

She removed her office attire and put on her fluffy pajamas. Her phone rang. If it was Terrance, she didn't want to hear any of his lies or excuses. But Charlotte's name flashed across the screen.

"How are you?" Charlotte asked when Mona answered.

"Let's just say I've had better weeks."

"Are you with Terrance or by yourself?"

"Being by myself is going to be the norm." Mona shared with Charlotte the scene at the office.

"I'm sorry to hear things aren't working out with you and Terrance."

"I knew it was too good to be true."

"Well, I hate to be the bearer of more bad news…"

"I got a big chocolate bar waiting for me, so go right ahead," Mona tried to joke, but barely mustered a laugh.

"Garrett was taken to the police station for questioning, but he has a good attorney so they didn't officially arrest him. Something about insufficient evidence. According to my friend at the police station, Garrett made you out to be a scorned ex who was bitter."

"I hate the day I ever laid eyes on Garrett!" Mona shouted. She hit the sofa pillow several times out of frustration.

"I can have Trevon, who's the owner of GT Securities, investigate more if you want."

Mona thought about it. She was ready to move completely on with her life. She didn't want anything else to do with Garrett. "Can you do me a favor? Can you have a message delivered to Garrett for me?"

"Sure, doll. Anything for my bestie."

"Inform him that if he ever contacts me, speaks to me, or reaches out to me in any form or fashion, I will expose him publicly."

"I can have Trevon do it as a courtesy, but be warned, it may not end up the way you want. It could have the opposite effect. Garrett might not take to threats too well."

Mona wasn't scared. "One thing that hasn't changed about Garrett is that he's all about his reputation. Even if I can't prove he drugged me, the mere fact he *could* be guilty will put a spot on his stellar reputation. He'll back off."

"Consider it handled. Anything else I can do for you?"

"Yes. Can you mend my broken heart?" Mona started bawling.

"After I handle this for you, I'm coming by." Charlotte ended the call.

Mona curled her legs under her in a ball on the sofa and cried tears of hurt and frustration.

Later on that night, Charlotte and Kem invaded Mona's place. They brought over pizza and more ice cream.

Mona wasn't used to having visitors. She was the one usually crashing at their place.

Kem said, "Where's the remote to the Apple TV? I'm ready to get the sappy movie watching over with."

"You write sappy stories but act like you don't want to watch them," Mona said.

Things were slowly getting back to normal. She and Kem were back to their friendly debating.

Four hours later, they were all snoring. Mona sat on one end of the couch and Charlotte on the other. Kem was laid out on a huge pillow on the floor.

A ringing cell phone woke them. "It's Sean," Charlotte said, looking at her screen. "I'm still at Mona's," she answered. "No, I don't need you to come get me. Kem will drop me off in the morning. Love you too."

"Since you're going to stay over, you two can have my bed and I'll sleep on the couch," Mona said once Charlotte had hung up.

Kem turned to her. "I'm fine right here on the floor."

"Girl, your couch will be even better if I can stretch my legs out," Charlotte added. "Go to bed. We'll be here in the morning."

Mona got off the couch and returned with two blankets. She handed them each one before returning to her bedroom.

Her phone was in the middle of the bed. She turned it on and saw she had several messages. Some were from Garrett. She could tell he was livid—the messages were crazy. She started to delete them, but then saved them just in case she needed them later on.

She laid the phone on the nightstand, feeling disappointed that Terrance still hadn't reached out to her.

At this point she was unable to sleep. She picked up her laptop from the nightstand and logged on to her 2-of-a-Kind account. She scrolled until she located the name Falcon. She saw his profile was still active, but he hadn't logged on recently.

She decided to send him a long message explaining her absence. She typed, *I hope you understand my disappearance had nothing to do with you. You've come across as a nice guy, so I'm reaching out to you as a friend. Maybe you can give me a different perspective, since you don't know me.*

She gave Falcon a brief overview on what had happened with Garrett, without using Garrett's name. She also shared how she'd gotten her heart broken recently by someone else and, at this point, didn't know if love was in the cards for her. *I wish you luck on finding your soul mate. You deserve a woman who can love you fully without the baggage.* She signed it *Raven*.

She felt better after confiding in the stranger. She logged out and was finally able to drift off to sleep.

Chapter Sixty-One

JERRICKA'S BUBBLY PERSONALITY GRATED ON Terrance's nerves. He felt like Scrooge. He didn't want to see other people happy when he was feeling so miserable. Losing Mona was like losing a part of himself. With his filming schedule, he didn't have the luxury of moping and hanging around at home. He had to push his feelings to the back of his mind and continue his duties.

He hoped Mona would remember that, regardless of what had happened with them, she had her obligations as well. He would give her the rest of the week to get herself together, but come Monday, she needed to report to the office every day. If she wasn't up to par, then he would have to make an executive decision and force her to do her job or be replaced. He'd lost her to Garrett, but he refused to lose the deal with the network.

Terrance's inbox was filled. Jerricka wasn't as fast as Mona at clearing out his email. He skimmed his messages, and his eyes stopped on an email from Raven via 2-of-a-Kind.

Terrance clicked on it. He wondered what Raven, also known as Mona, had to say to his alter ego, Falcon.

He read the message, then hit the desk with his fist. Garrett had tried to rape her. Terrance could kick himself, because he'd seen them that night. Mona had needed him, but he'd let his pride and ego get in the way and left her to fend for herself. Thankfully, she got away from him unharmed—but what if she hadn't?

Terrance called her number. Charlotte answered. "May I speak to Mona?" he asked.

"I'm sorry, Terrance, but she doesn't feel like talking to you right now."

"Tell her it's important."

He heard Charlotte mention his name to Mona but couldn't hear her response.

Charlotte got back on the line. "Is it work related?"

"No. It's personal."

"It's personal," Charlotte yelled. There was a pause before she said, "She said if it's not business related, she can't talk."

Terrance sighed. "Fine. Tell her I will see her bright and early Monday morning."

He didn't wait for Charlotte to deliver his message. He disconnected.

How could he have been so *stupid?* He'd given up on their relationship too fast. He could only imagine what Mona thought of him. And she'd heard him tell his mom he was ready to move on.

Terrance's head pounded. The intensity of the pain was so strong, it felt like someone had used a hammer to bang a nail in his forehead. He reached into his desk drawer and pulled out some aspirin. The bottle recommended two, but he took three. He swallowed the pills with a bottle of water.

He needed his head to stop hurting. He couldn't think clearly.

Jerricka called via the intercom, "You have a call on line one."

"Who is it?" he asked.

"Sean Maxwell."

"I'll take it." Terrance hit the button on the phone. "Sean, just the man I need to talk to. I need a favor. A huge one."

"Anything for you, man."

Terrance enlisted Sean's help in winning back his woman. Now if he could only get Mona to talk to him…

He logged on to his 2-of-a-Kind profile and sent a response to her.

Raven, I think you're a remarkable woman. I'm sorry you've gone through so much since the last time we chatted. I want to make things right with you for not meeting you that night. Are you available to meet me tomorrow night at seven p.m. at the Studio in Laguna Beach? I will go ahead and make the reservations. After all you've been through, you deserve the royal treatment.

Terrance hit the send button, then called the restaurant to reserve a private dining room. It cost him extra due to the last-minute reservation, but he didn't care.

He could barely work due to his checking his email constantly, waiting for Mona's response.

He held his breath when he saw Raven's name appear. He opened the email.

I will be there wearing black. Who should I ask for?

Terrance exhaled. "Yes!" He typed, *Ask for Falcon. The maître d' will escort you to my table.*

Mona responded, *Falcon, it will be great to finally meet you. Thanks for listening to my long rant.*

That's what friends are for. Until tomorrow. Terrance signed the name *Falcon* and logged off.

Jerricka's voice came across the intercom again. "Your mom's on the phone. She calls you every day, doesn't she?"

Terrance laughed. Some young people had no filter, he thought. "Just send the call through." He picked up. "Mom, before you go into your spiel, there's something I want to tell you."

"You're going after Mona again, aren't you?"

"Yes. It's been a big misunderstanding on my part, and now it's on me to fix it."

"What do you mean?" Sara asked.

Terrance explained to his mother what he'd learned. "So, Mona wasn't choosing Garrett over me. He'd forced his way into her life. All of this could have ended tragically, but thank God it didn't."

Silence. Sara didn't say a word.

"Mom. Are you there?"

"If she's the woman you want, then you have my support."

Terrance needed to make sure he'd heard her correctly. "What did you say?"

She repeated herself, then continued, "So, how do you plan on getting her to speak to you, let alone proposing to her?"

"Let's just say I have a virtual friend helping me out."

"Whatever that means. Keep me posted. Love you."

Terrance felt like another weight had been lifted from his shoulders. Having his mom's support meant more to him than she would ever know.

Chapter Sixty-Two

MONA HAD HEARD OF THE Studio at Laguna Beach, but this would be her first time going there for dinner. She didn't even mind the hour drive to get there. It would give her time to clear her head. If she could find an inexpensive hotel, she was considering spending the night at the beach.

Although she had no romantic desires for Falcon, she still wanted to look her best. She pinned her hair in a bun and wore an emerald necklace and matching earrings. She slipped on a black fitted knee-length dress. The see-through Cinderella-style pumps rounded out her outfit.

Her cell phone beeped. It was Charlotte. *Sean and I wanted to do something special for you. We're sending a car to get you and drive you wherever you want to go.*

She responded, *Thanks. Perfect timing. I was about to head out now.*

Charlotte responded, *Look out your window. The car should be waiting for you.*

Mona went to her window and saw a stretch limousine in front of the neighbor's yard. She could see a few neighbors standing in their doorways gawking.

She didn't want an audience, but if she was going to make it on time for her date, she needed to leave now.

She grabbed her purse, locked the door, and headed down the stairs. Mona felt like a superstar as the neighbors stared.

"Ms. Johnson?" the limousine driver asked.

"Yes."

He held the door open for her, and she entered. "Where to?" he asked before closing the door.

"Studio in Laguna Beach."

"I know exactly where it is," he responded, before closing the door.

Mona looked out the window and saw her neighbors watch them drive away. She was glad Charlotte and Sean had gotten the car for her. Instead of having to deal with traffic, it gave her time to think.

The two times she'd fallen in love had both ended in disaster. Coincidentally, both men's mothers hadn't liked her.

Thoughts of Terrance filled her mind. She smiled as she remembered the fun times they'd shared. But her smile turned into a frown. She was still beating herself up about not telling Terrance what had happened with Garrett. Maybe if she had, things would be different.

Despite what she'd done, she still couldn't believe Terrance had decided to move on without even telling her. When was he going to talk to her? When he and the new woman were on their honeymoon?

She tried to think back to where she'd gone wrong. Didn't Terrance know he was her everything? Without him, she felt empty. She wanted to reach out to him. If Charlotte hadn't answered her phone yesterday, she probably would have talked to him.

She needed to know why. Was it because he thought she was seeing Garrett? He had to know by now Garrett meant nothing to her.

The limousine driver opened the partition. "We're about five minutes away."

"Thanks." Mona used a napkin from the bar and wiped the tears from her eyes and cheeks. She removed the compact mirror from her clutch and reapplied some of her makeup.

She'd just put on another layer of lipstick when the limousine pulled in front of the five-star resort hotel and restaurant located on the beachfront.

Mona reached inside her purse to tip the driver. He refused to take it. "My tip's already taken care of." He handed Mona a card. "When you're ready to go, just give me a call. I'll be around here somewhere."

She slipped the card into her clutch and went inside of the restaurant. Everything was trimmed in gold. The place was packed, and if you didn't have a reservation, more than likely you wouldn't be getting a seat.

"I'm a guest of Falcon," Mona told the maître d'.

"Of course. You must be Raven. He told me to expect you."

Mona followed the maître d' through the restaurant. He opened the door to a private room. "Your host is already here. He will be in shortly. In the meantime, enjoy some hors d'oeuvres and the live music."

Mona entered the room, which looked like a dining room with a fireplace. The table was set for two with fine china, and in the center was a bottle of champagne sitting in a silver container of ice. The curtains were opened, revealing a stunning Southern California ocean view. She stared out the window.

"It's breathtaking, isn't it? Just like you."

Mona turned around and came face to face with the last person she'd expected to see. "Terrance, what are you doing here?"

"I thought you would have figured it out by now. I'm Falcon."

"No, you can't be..." Mona trailed off. The more she thought back to her online conversations with Falcon, the more she recognized some similarities.

"I *am* Falcon, and I've been a fool." Terrance walked over to her and got on one knee. "Mona, please forgive me."

"Terrance, I don't know. So many things have happened." Her hand flew to her mouth. "Oh my goodness. I told Falcon about Garrett. I can't believe I was foolish enough to tell a stranger all of my business. I said things I should have been telling you instead. Can *you* forgive *me*?"

He stood and took Mona's hand. "Of course. Baby, all of this has been one big misunderstanding. I thought you chose Garrett."

"You should have come to me. I would have told you everything you needed to know." Mona's hand shook.

"Imagine seeing you hugged up with Garrett, looking like a loving couple on their way to a hotel room to end their night on a high note…"

Mona chuckled. "Only a producer would paint a scene like that."

He kissed her open palm. "I've been a fool. The only way I knew to get you to come was to use Falcon."

"What about the woman your mom was trying to introduce you to? If that was nothing, why didn't you come after me?"

"At that point, I felt like I'd already lost you. My stupid pride held me back."

Sean Maxwell's voice could be heard. Mona looked through the door and saw Sean standing in front of the band singing one of his love ballads. "Will you take my hand…make me a better man… and go with me?"

Terrance led Mona out on the terrace. "Look over there." He pointed.

She saw a huge banner in the moonlit sky with *Mona, will you marry me?* written on it.

She looked back at Terrance, speechless.

He kneeled again, took a box from his pocket, and held it out. "Mona, I don't want to go another day without you knowing how much I love you. Will you do me the honor and the privilege of becoming my wife?"

Mona couldn't believe it. She loved Terrance, but one thing held her back from saying yes.

Terrance could feel his heart falling. She hadn't responded. Sean continued to sing a tender ballad in the background.

Terrance stood. Tears fell from Mona's eyes.

"Your mother doesn't like me. I know how much you love your mother, and I don't want to be the cause of a rift between you two. I wouldn't be able to forgive myself." She looked away.

"My mom's given me her blessing," Terrance said.

"She did what?" Mona sounded shocked.

"She knows I'm here proposing to you. She's not going to stand in our way. She knows you're the woman I want to be with."

Mona took the ring box from Terrance and held it open. "Are you going to put this ring on my finger or not?"

"So is it a yes?" Terrance wanted to make sure. He didn't want any more misunderstandings between them.

"Yes, Terrance. Yes, I will marry you."

He slipped the ring on her finger. "I love you, Mona. Don't ever doubt it."

She stared into his eyes. "I love you. Don't *you* ever forget it."

Terrance wrapped his arm around Mona's waist and devoured her lips. They got lost in each other, not caring that they had an audience.

Cheers could be heard from behind them.

They turned to see Sean and Charlotte in the doorway. Mona looked at Terrance and laughed.

Charlotte and Sean came out on the terrace. Mona held out the ring so Charlotte could admire the six-carat emerald-cut diamond.

"You're my best friend, and you know I don't like surprises." Mona playfully hit Charlotte on the arm.

"I knew you would like this one." Charlotte winked.

Sean stood next to Charlotte. "We're going to leave you two alone."

"Thanks, Sean, for making this a memorable night," Mona said.

"You're my girl." He hugged her.

Charlotte and Sean left. Mona looked into Terrance's loving eyes. "What a year this has been," she said.

Terrance wrapped his around her waist again. "The year I discovered the meaning of true love."

"Terrance, I plan on spending the rest of my life showing you how much I love and adore you," Mona said.

"I will always love and adore you too, my sunshine." Terrance kissed Mona's lips and eased his tongue inside of her mouth as the moon shone brightly over the ocean.

ACKNOWLEDGMENTS

This book would not exist without the love and support of so many people. I am deeply grateful to my mother, my brothers, my sisters-in-laws, my aunts, uncles, cousins and friends for their constant encouragement, patience, and belief in me.

My sincere thanks to my agent and publisher for their guidance, support, and commitment to bringing these stories to life. Your professionalism and belief in my work mean more than words can express.

To my readers, thank you for showing up, spreading the word, and continuing to support my books. Every message, review, and recommendation matters more than you know. To the Writer Boss Babes community, thank you for the inspiration, encouragement, and shared belief in creative women owning their voices and their stories.

Stories may begin on the page, but they shine because of the people who believe in them.

With gratitude,

Shelia Goss

ABOUT THE AUTHOR

Shelia M. Goss is a national bestselling and award-winning author known for her captivating romance novels and dynamic storytelling. With over twenty-one books to her name, including the *Essence Magazine* bestselling *My Invisible Husband* and the critically acclaimed *The Joneses*, Shelia has earned praise for her emotionally rich characters and plot twists. *USA Today* praised her, saying, *"Goss has an easy, flowing style with her prose."* An AAMBC Romance Author of the Year and Library Journal Best Books honoree, she is also the creator of the Women in Hollywood collection, which explores love, ambition, and the personal cost of life in the spotlight, beginning with Worth the Risk. Shelia continues to leave her mark in both the literary and screenwriting worlds. While her work spans multiple genres, romance remains her heart and passion. Visit her online at www.sheliagoss.com.